PRAISE FOR *NECESSARY DEEDS*

"What makes *Necessary Deeds* so irresistible and addictive is that it's a devilishly inventive murder mystery presented in the finest of sentences and filtered through a mind wonderfully beset at every turn by the dark truths of human desire, ambition, envy, and jealousy—but most of all by love itself. If Mark Wish's life imitates his art, his gift for storytelling might just get him murdered. But not before his next book deal, please. In any case, *Necessary Deeds* is a necessary read."

—Tim Johnston, *New York Times* bestselling author of *Descent* and *Distant Sons*

"By turns tense and tender, Mark Wish's *Necessary Deeds* delivers a high-stakes noir and a taut tale of jealousy, murder, and redemption."

—Laura McHugh, internationally bestselling author of *The Weight of Blood*

"*Necessary Deeds* is a tight, tense thriller that explores some of the darkest, twistiest workings of the human mind. Mark Wish asks the question: Who can you trust if you can't trust yourself?"

—Lou Berney, winner of Edgar, Hammet, Anthony, Dagger, and ALA Awards, author of *November Road*

"Mark Wish's *Necessary Deeds* hits the sweet spot: sly, sharp, and satirical. Highly entertaining!"

—Alan Orloff, Anthony, Agatha, Derringer, and two-time Thriller Award winning author

"Smart and gripping, nuanced and wryly observed, *Necessary Deeds* is unputdownable, and Wish is clearly a writer at the top of his game. A phenomenal thriller that will leave you breathless."

—Tish Cohen, author of *The Summer We Lost Her*

"Bursting at the seams with voice and tension, Mark Wish's *Necessary Deeds* reads like the literary lovechild of Bellow, Chandler and Robert Bolaño. This is a literary page-turner, full of life and poetry. A novel to be devoured, then savored."

—Daniel Torday, two-time winner of the National Jewish Book Award, author of *The Last Flight of Poxl West*

"In *Necessary Deeds'* Matt Connell, Mark Wish has created a diabolically compelling anti-hero—a literary agent with both romance and murder in his heart. As soon as I read the first few lines of this novel, I was all the way in—Wish portrays the high-stakes New York City literary world and the conflicted soul of Connell with humor, pathos, and supreme suspense."

—Grace Paley Prize winner Christine Sneed, author of *Little Known Facts*

"Smart, exceptionally told, and a pleasure to read, this mystery by Mark Wish is complemented by dialogue brimming with emotional insights, whether about the foreboding passion between a man and a woman, or the rage of a wounded husband. *Necessary Deeds* is the kind of book you read in a rush but remember long after."

—E. A. Aymar, bestselling author of *No Home for Killers*

"I was hooked by the first sentence—one of the best I've read—and followed Mark Wish's tale on and on. Wish knows how to tell a story, and in *Necessary Deeds*, he has given us a varied, surprising, and irresistibly engaging one."

—Pulitzer Prize winner Tim Page, author of *Parallel Play*

"*Necessary Deeds* is a captivating, spiraling story that doesn't let up off the throttle. When it was over, I found myself wanting—no, needing—that speed again. Wish has created a stunning narrative with so much drive and power. Any reader would love this."

—PEN Award winner Morgan Talty, national bestselling author of *Night of the Living Rez*

"*Necessary Deeds* is a rarity: a murder mystery that keeps you guessing until the very end, and most important, is a lot of fun. Mark Wish has written a witty page-turner that's necessary reading."

—Leland Cheuk, author of *No Good Very Bad Asian*

"Mark Wish's *Necessary Deeds* is a deliciously gleeful send-up of the New York literary world, a wildly satirical removal of the veil over High Art. Most notably, it's a genuine whodunnit: Who is murdering the Talented Writers in the city (with their outsized advances)? Intertwined throughout is a noir love story and humor, but also a clear-eyed gaze at what has happened to notions of Integrity, Literature…and Fame. The twist at the end took me by surprise while making perfect wicked sense."

—Drue Heinz Literature Prize winner Katherine Vaz, author of *Fado and Other Stories*

NECESSARY DEEDS

Mark Wish

Regal House Publishing

Published by
Regal House Publishing, LLC
Raleigh, NC 27605
All rights reserved

ISBN -13 (paperback): 9781646034062
ISBN -13 (epub): 9781646034079
Library of Congress Control Number: 2023934859

Cover design by © C. B. Royal

"Hope" by Mark Wish, first published by *The Iowa Review*.
Reprinted with permission.

Regal House Publishing, LLC
https://regalhousepublishing.com

The following is a work of fiction created by the author. All names, individuals, characters, places, items, brands, events, etc., were either the product of the author or were used fictitiously. Any name, place, event, person, brand, or item, current or past, is entirely coincidental.

Printed in the United States of America

For my father, who taught me the joy of loving words. Had hoped this one would appear in print while you were still around, Dad. Rest in peace knowing lyrics and phrases of yours "came through."

1

ere in Sing Sing, the killers I've met are better story-
tellers than most of the novelists I've represented.
They'll bombard you with twists and turns about how
they were ambushed and shackled and prosecuted harshly despite their innocence, and you'll find yourself nodding, buying
their horror stories.

To be fair, though, I should probably admit that I'm naturally more inclined to suspend disbelief for these guys—my fellow
inmates—because of my need to get along with them. After
all, for years now I've wanted to prove to Warden Scardina that
the stint of fury in which I myself killed a human being was a
singular incident in an otherwise placid life. I mean, I'm trying
to convince him I deserve an early release. Or at least inclusion
on the list of exemplary inmates whose hours in the yard have
been tripled.

In fact I'm out there, in the yard, when I first meet Jonas. On
the unshaded basketball court, where my mood often spikes
if direct sunshine finds me. Using the hoop with no net and
therefore alone, sometimes lost in thought about my victim,
sometimes imagining him putting his first move on my ex, in
any case vulnerable to the whims of anyone who has the nerve
to approach me.

And Jonas indeed has the nerve. As he crosses the out-of-
bounds line, all I know about him (well, all I've heard about him
since he arrived here yesterday) is that he, too, has killed a man,
in his case during a flubbed attempt to rob the Mahopac OTB
while partnering up with a defective AR-15.

"This hoop yours?" is how he starts with me.

"Usually."

"You play in school?"

I hoist up a shot that proves to be a brick. "Just out here for the vitamin D."

He folds his arms, studies me up and down. To imply I fear no one, I reciprocate. I see a gaunt, slightly hunched yet taut fellow ten years younger than I and six inches taller. I see a clean-shaven horse face, a weak yet cleft chin. Green eyes that squint a little through black hornrims, a full head of brown hair with gray coming in barely and on the sides only.

Mine, by the way, went completely white during my first five months here.

"How long you in for?" I ask.

"Would rather not discuss that."

I pass him the ball, which he bobbles. He does not shoot. My guess is he doesn't give a shit about hoop either.

"Would rather hear what you know about Ethan Hendee," he says.

Ethan Hendee was a client of mine who, eighteen years ago—that is, more than a decade before I learned my wife wasn't exactly a saint—gave up on writing novels to write poems that appear in those photocopied literary mags no one reads. He's a helluva writer, candid and interesting and succinct as anyone published, but I have not survived here by not holding cards close. So: "Ethan Hendee?"

"Ha."

"Why ha?"

"Because I know you're Matthew Connell, and that you've represented the poet Ethan Hendee for a long time."

"The only problem being I don't know such a person."

"But see, bro, there's no question in my mind that you do know him. I know you've been his agent for years."

I shake my head no. Eye the asphalt between us and the cyclone fence.

"You trying to tell me you're not Matthew Connell?" he asks.

"*Matt* Connell." I force a sour expression. "Maybe you're confusing me with some hoity-toity guy? Anyway, how does someone who hauls around an AR-15 know anything about poetry?"

He points at his hornrims. "Because he's read some?"

"Well, I don't know any Hendee."

"But see, Matt, I still think you do. Plus I think that, as his literary agent, you know what a badass he is."

In all truth, I do not know this. The Ethan Hendee I represented before my arrest had a soul gentle as any. I'm curious about what this Jonas guy heard Hendee did, but to get an early release, I've pledged to myself never to talk about crime that's gone down on the outside. After all, a rehabbed convict no longer cares about crime, and I am nothing if not a rehabbed convict.

To let this Jonas guy know I'm done socializing for the day, I turn and face the run of the Hudson beyond the chain link and the razor wire, its waves peaking into whitecaps here and there.

"So you're not gonna spill?" he asks.

I don't as much as shrug.

He zings me a no-look pass, really zips it, hard, straight at my head, but I notice it soon enough to catch it.

"Ya missed," I mutter loud enough for him to hear, and I look over to stare him down, but his back is already turned, a confident stride taking him off.

And it occurs to me, as he heads to the guarded double doors between us and the inside, that if he doesn't have six inches on me, he has seven.

And that my own storied past has taught me that the strength to kill a man comes not only from size—it also comes from youth.

So I'll avoid him, I decide. Won't let him know I'm avoiding him, but that's what I'll do.

There's an art to this.

I spend the rest of my time in the yard pretending I care only about my jump shot. At one point I miss sixteen straight. I admit to myself that if this Jonas wanted to get inside my head, well, he has. And as I continue to miss generally, I think more about Ethan Hendee. How does a sixty-some-year-old recluse who's devoted his life to writing poems suddenly leave his hovel of a basement apartment to do something awful enough to be known by a guy like Jonas?

I ponder this question on and off even after I'm back in my cell. At dinner I ignore Jonas's glances at me from two tables over, letting my stone-cold expression announce my resolve to keep to myself. Assuring him we'll never be friends, pals, partners, whatever you want to call it. I am done trusting anyone male. Probably I'm done trusting anyone.

I sleep fitfully that night, with Lauren invading my thoughts only slightly more than Hendee does. More than once I try to dismiss the moment I learned she'd been with a man whose literary success I made happen. Conjuring my state of mind during the twenty-eight minutes that followed that moment can trip off a replay of that state (the uncontrollable acceleration of thoughts, the sharp panic due to loss of control, the gouging sense that my very personhood has been decimated), and I don't want such a replay. I want to be calm. I need calm to sleep. I must sleep so I can conduct myself admirably next I see a guard.

Finally, I doze. Somewhat and for who knows how long. I wake to the clinks of a guard's keys unlocking my cell. There's another guard with him, a younger one, maybe a rookie. The older one mutters, "Scardina wants to see you."

Scardina's presence in the building means it must be 8:00 a.m. at least. I get up, splash my face with the trickle I conjure from my tiny faucet, rake back my hair with my fingertips, hear the younger guard say, "This ain't a beauty pageant, bro." He cuffs me, and they both flank me, and we all three are off.

Scardina is a thick, serene-looking man with a decent array of suits thanks to his status as head warden, an apparently favorite pair of brown wing-tipped shoes, and hands he's kept palms-down on his desk whenever he's had me in his office. Eight months after I arrived in this mecca of repentance, he took advantage of my experience as a literary agent by hav-

ing me revise his memoir gratis, the gratis part being his idea.
On the theory that you never tell your warden how boring his
writing is, I merely addressed his whimsical use of commas (he
was clueless about when to use them and when not to) and
jotted him a list of forty agents I'd competed with before my
twenty-eight minutes. I told him to mention me in queries to
these agents—that is, if he felt my name wasn't mud. All forty
turned him down with form rejections, doubtless because his
398 double-spaced pages narrated only his coming of age, the
climax of which was a hike he and his father took resulting in
their discovery of a raspberry patch.

Today, though, Scardina's life story will take a jolting twist—
at least in the eyes of yours truly. Today is the day after Jonas
approached me in the yard, and Scardina, wearing a periwinkle
blue suit and a silver and black tie striped downward and to the
right if you face it, sits up straighter at his desk as a guard leads
me in. Today Scardina's hands are folded, as if he's praying.
He does not acknowledge me. His gaze is on the floor. On the
folding chair between me and the window that overlooks the
Hudson and Jersey, in a gray suit and thin black tie and holding
a smartphone large as any I've seen, sits Jonas sans the horn-
rimmed glasses.

"Jonas," I say.

"Matthew," Jonas says, smirking slightly.

"It's Matt, bro," I say.

"Whatever," he says.

Scardina clears his throat. Jonas merely watches me. Jonas
appears more hunched than he did in the yard.

And older.

And smarter, which scares me.

"Matt, I haven't exactly been forthright with you," he finally
says. "So let me fill you in on something: I'm with the FBI."

Learning I've been deceived always trips off that state of
mind I suffered during my twenty-eight minutes, and this time
the acceleration of thoughts is accompanied by a shockingly
quick spike of heat in my head, far more than your face feels

when you blush. I try to appear collected and docile, however—
because, of course, Scardina is watching me.

"And I want you to read this," Jonas says, and he swipes a
sheet of paper off Scardina's desk and hands it to me.

What's on it is a xeroxed published poem written by—here
he is again—Ethan Hendee. Because I've never managed to sell
a book manuscript of Hendee's to a publisher in the city (or
anywhere, for that matter), Hendee has, on his own, gotten so
many poems into the little mags I've lost count—for all I know
by now, he's up to 4,000.

I read this one slowly, to give myself time to guess Jonas's
angle in showing it to me:

A Quieter Saturday Night

of those 2 grandparents
my grandmother was nicer
but she loved my brother so much
there was rarely laughter in her
for me & on that night my
brother wasn't there—it was just the 2
of us & my grandfather
& my grandfather never spoke so it
felt as if it were just
the 2 of us
she & I were playing
cards for nickels & she was
winning & my grandfather was reading
the paper & I could tell
she liked to win but it bothered her she'd
lent me the nickels
in the first place
it just wasn't the same for her:
winning at cards with this grandson
who didn't like nuns
it would be better if she

were winning against adults & their money
or even losing to my brother
who she was sure would
become a priest
& he did become a priest—
after she
died
then he
died from a virus
he caught from a priest
& the last 2 things
I'd do tonight are
go to church
& play cards
my grandfather died
also but by then I was no longer
around to see him off
still I am him in this room: full
of words
not saying
any of them

Hendee's candor has touched my heart yet again, but I decide that, for the moment, it's best to appear unfazed. I stand, shrug, place the poem on Scardina's desk.

"You know who wrote that thing, right?" Jonas asks.

"No," I say.

"It said so on the header."

"Guess I missed that."

"Matt, your client Ethan Hendee wrote that poem."

"I wouldn't say Hendee's my client."

"I would. And there's plenty of evidence to prove me right."

"Is that so?"

"All sorts back at my headquarters."

Headquarters. God, do I love that word. As an agent—that is, before my twenty-eight minutes—I always wanted a headquarters, an airy square footage in which like-minded colleagues and I could find repose. Where I'd gain moral support and refresh my resolve on the toughest days in the grand competition that is publishing.

This is also why I've helped most of my clients rewrite the books I've represented: I've enjoyed working with people to forge something better than what either of us could make on our own.

Come to think of it, this was also why I got married.

And only now, after having survived here in Sing Sing for four years, thirty-three weeks, and twelve days, do I accept wholly my deceased mother's belief that, as she'd often say after my father left and all she had was me, "Happiness depends on who you're with." Lauren, my ex, was who I was with pretty much twenty-four seven during my marriage, making me pretty much always happy, so when my client Blaine Davis told me, over lunch, that Lauren had taken a lover—and that this lover was my client and pal Geoff Considine—well, processing those truths all at once was clearly too much of an ask. I sensed, as I soon thereafter stormed over to Considine's apartment in the East Village, that what I wanted to do was horrible and the sort of thing that puts even the kindest man behind bars, but something in me felt doing it was necessary more than it was wrong. I *knew* it was wrong, but never once during those crucial twenty-eight minutes of my life did I feel the wrongness of doing it. Not as I shouted all manner of obscenity-laced threats at Considine so loudly my throat went raw, not as I grabbed him by the shoulders and tossed him sideways so hard he mewed like a child as he hit the hardwood floor. Not as my hands were twisting his neck long after his Adam's apple clicked, not even after the capillaries in the whites of his eyes burst and turned them pink. And then, of course, it was too late: I was a killer, just like Hendee might be a killer if that's what Jonas meant when he called him a badass.

"Matt?" Scardina is saying. "You okay?"

"Absolutely."

"So I'm to take it you're admitting to being Ethan Hendee's agent?"

Again, I go tongue-tied. This time it's because, one, I still can't believe Hendee did something the FBI would care about, and, two, if he has, I need for Scardina to know I've played no part in whatever he did.

"Never lie to the FBI, bro," Jonas is saying, maybe condescendingly, maybe kiddingly. A mole the width of a #2 pencil eraser is on a side of his neck, but I'm not thinking about wringing that neck. I'm not thinking about hurting anyone.

I'm thinking about the Lauren I sometimes consider the *real* Lauren, the woman I knew when I asked her to marry me.

"You should know that from all the crime novels you've sold," Jonas adds.

"The thing is," I say, "I have absolutely no reason to believe Hendee still considers me his agent."

And in my mind at least, I do sound calm. Measured. Like a person who oughta be back in the city hunting down heartfelt manuscripts and getting them into print.

"Why's that?" Jonas asks.

"Because I'm *here,* man. I mean, if I couldn't sell Hendee's work before my conviction, how would I sell it while I'm behind bars?"

Scardina is staring me down.

"Anyway, so I once represented him?" I ask, my question aimed half at Scardina. "I mean, seriously, what difference does it make?"

I hope Scardina understands that, even if I am challenging Jonas, I am, by troubleshooting his logic, more or less helping the FBI.

"Not to mention," I tell Jonas, "I never submitted that poem anywhere for the guy. I mean, if you did your homework, you'd know that essentially no literary agent submits individual poems."

"Why is that?" Scardina asks.

"No dough in it."

Scardina leans back in his wide pleather chair, cocks his head as if, in the wake of those four words—*No dough in it*—he's banishing a fantasy to become the next Robert Frost.

Jonas says, "Just for the record, Matt: you are indeed admitting that you have, at least at some point in time, represented Ethan Hendee, correct?"

I ask him, "And what if I did?"

He grimaces. "Okay, here's the deal, my friend. Three young women, all debut novelists recently signed by major publishing houses in Manhattan, have gone missing, and severed pieces of their corpses have been found floating in the East River, starting with their right hands. Their *right* hands, Matt. The ones they signed their contracts with."

Again, my thoughts accelerate. This time both my head and my neck go feverish, severely so, the heat now radiating down into my shoulders, my chest. Maybe this is because, in my experience, publishing has always been loaded with envy and anger, and I've always disliked this reality but have generally gone along with it. Maybe because I should've known something so violent would happen sooner or later among NYC's literati and should've tried to prevent it long ago. I don't know for sure why it is, and the fact that I don't know closes my throat and causes my mouth to salivate.

Jonas is saying, "And the reason I'm sitting here is a slew of FBI agents, not to mention detectives at NYPD, are having a hell of a time tracing down the offending monster, who the tabloids are calling the Success Killer. And since all three of the victims were novelists, and female, and young, the FBI's best theory is that Ethan Hendee is this monster."

A house editor I used to lunch with once called Hendee a "bad boy"—though for reasons I never asked about—so I'm shocked, but not completely.

"I mean, let's face it, Matt: Hendee is getting old, and he *is* a loner," Jonas continues. "And most every writer in the city the Bureau has talked to has characterized him as edgy if not downright angry."

"And these people have based this assessment of theirs on what?" I ask.

"Having a gut feeling about his work, a funny feeling when they've met him personally, things like that. Of course most of us at the Bureau don't find having a bad rep as being particularly conclusive, but the thing is, Matt, to a person, every writer we talked to mentioned Hendee first when we asked which writer in the city disturbed them most."

"Of course they did. He's been published hundreds of times more than they have. He's international."

"Yet he's never had a book published."

"True."

"So our top criminal psychologist says that this irony itself, Matt, goes straight to Hendee's motive. I mean, let's face it: Here the guy's been writing for almost thirty years—after having been told by you, the kickass agent you were back then, that he has major-league talent—and he is, as you put it, international, but now he's in a situation in which, financially speaking, he'd be better off lying on Columbus Circle beside a paper cup. And then he hears about these women—*young* women not even twenty-five years old!—and *three* of them!—and they all three are not only flaunting seven-fig, two-book deals for novels they've yet to finish drafting, they're also getting film options without batting an eye."

I let what I'm hearing sink in. The possibility that Hendee could have felt such severe envy troubles me, but I still can't believe he's the Success Killer. I know killers, more than a few. It will never not be true that I am one. And after all these days and nights I've spent on only sixty square feet of concrete, I believe I know to the core the killer I once was, and Hendee is nothing like him.

"Listen," I say to Jonas. "Hendee, as I knew him, never got upset about anyone else's success. When he'd hear I landed a book deal for another client of mine, he'd email me things like, 'Good to know we're still in the game'—then simply return to writing more poems."

"So you're saying you don't think he envied the three women."

"Not the Hendee I knew."

"Our top head doctor is saying Hendee did envy them but pretended not to. And that this made for a cauldron of motivation, if you will."

Scardina, I realize, is reading "A Quieter Saturday Night." With a glance up at Jonas, he asks, "Your crime shrink notice his failure to use punctuation?"

Jonas nods.

"And you figure this goes to Hendee's problems with authority?" Scardina asks.

"It doesn't suggest he plays by the rules."

"But gentlemen," I say. "Hendee's a poet. A poet's supposed to question authority."

"Except no other widely published poet is doing it without punctuation," Jonas says. "At least not incessantly in thousands of poems, many of which, our top head doctor has noted, take jabs at authority explicitly."

"Who is this guy, anyway—this head doctor?" I ask.

"It's a woman, Matt. Name's Dawn Trinko. In any event, if you ask me personally, as not only an undercover agent but also as a plain old human being—and one who actually does read poetry now and then—I'd tell you that poems like this one of Hendee's we're looking at here represent a cry for help."

"Uh-huh," I say, trying to keep my tone from sounding dubious.

"Not to mention," Scardina says, "if we go by this poem, the guy still harbors a fairly intense dislike of his grandmother. I mean, who doesn't like their *grandmother*? I mean, hello? Some issues with women maybe?"

I get up and walk over to Scardina and nod at "A Quieter Saturday Night," and he hands it to me, and I stand in front of his desk rereading it.

Okay, I think. He didn't put Grandma in the very best light.

But this is a *poem*, I think. A mortal, godforsaken poem.

"Even if this is autobiographical," I say, handing the sheet back to Scardina, "I see it as mourning the loss of a brother, and maybe of family in general, more than I see it as hatred of anyone."

"You're saying it's not autobiographical?" Jonas asks.

"I'm saying Hendee never told me he had a brother who died."

Scardina's eyes leave mine to land on Jonas, who raises his chin slightly.

"Well, he did, Matt," Jonas says. "An older brother whose death, from what we understand, was not a pretty thing. Our understanding, from the interviews we've conducted, is that Hendee's inability to focus on work for long periods of time after this brother's death is why he turned to writing poems rather than writing novels. Which, as you point out, meant his own writing career was pretty much bound to go nowhere if you measure a career by lucrative book deals and number of copies sold. So, sure, maybe his brother's death excuses some of his frustration and anger, but it doesn't give him the right to kill people, let alone dismember them. I mean, everyone has deaths in their families. And everyone feels sorrow—it's how life goes. And maybe some of us have had grandparents who didn't favor us, or who were, for that matter, batshit crazy. But that doesn't mean we get to go around murdering young women who've done absolutely nothing wrong."

I gaze at the stretch of the Hudson visible through Scardina's window.

"And the fact that he didn't tell you he had a brother who died, Matt, is further proof that he's a secret-keeper—that he's capable of living a double life."

Jesus, I think. Hendee?

"In any case, bro," Jonas says, "let me get to what I've been sent here to do. The Bureau has arranged for your release on parole—provided you go undercover with me to get enough evidence on Hendee to establish probable cause and make an arrest."

Release, I think. I'm so shocked all I can think to say is, "You and *I* make the arrest?"

"You would be yourself, a formerly well-respected literary agent, out of here early for good behavior. I'd be a wannabe author from California who's moved to the city because, while you were in here, you received letters from me that proved I had so much talent you wanted to represent me as soon as you got out."

I'm blinking repeatedly at Jonas despite trying to appear professional.

"But I'd never do that," I say.

"You will now if you want an early release."

"But I don't think...I can't honestly tell you I believe Hendee's guilty."

"But you agree it's *possible* he is."

Hendee, I realize, has never visited me here. I shrug.

"And the Bureau, Matt, is in the business of knowing who's guilty. What I'm saying is, with all due respect to you and your accomplishments as a literary agent before you...lost your temper, what you're looking at from me presently is a take-it-or-leave-it proposition. And the offer ends..." Jonas glances at his watch. "In three minutes."

My thoughts again begin to accelerate. Is it possible Hendee was never the gentleman I took him to be? Or that he was kindhearted for years but at some point unbeknownst to me slipped into bitterness? Was I so mesmerized by the seemingly candid lines he typed I went blind to the sociopath who'd been typing them?

Again, I'm blinking repeatedly. I need to say something to slow down my mind, so I ask Scardina, "And you're okay with this?"

"As long as you help the Bureau make the arrest."

"See, we can't get a warrant, Matt," Jonas tells me. "Not even a search warrant. Magistrate has the same notions you do, about the opinions of a guy's colleagues and a few lines in his poems not being enough to establish probable cause."

"But the Bureau thinks the magistrate's wrong," I say.

"We *know* he's wrong. Recently we've learned from a friend of mine at ConEd that the usage of electricity in Hendee's basement apartment in Chinatown is unaccountably high. That is, unless he's running a couple of decent-sized freezers down there."

"I don't understand."

"Our theory, Matt, is that, after Hendee woos these female novelists with his beleaguered poet shtick and kills them, he keeps his place free of the stench of decomposing flesh by freezing them. That is, while he's steadily cutting them into pieces small enough to walk one by one to the East River."

"So if I don't find freezers in his place, I end up right back in here."

"No-no," Jonas says. "You might also find a hair. Or a personal belonging of one of the victims, or, ideally, blood. And you'll wear a wire anytime you're in his vicinity."

"Because you think he'll tell me something?"

"It's our sense, Matt, that if he'll tell anyone something, it would be you. We also believe that with you having just been released from here—with your supposedly new lease on life and all—he might feel renewed hope in your ability to sell a book of his, in which case he'd probably share some of his most recent writing with you. Which Trinko says has an eighty-nine percent chance of including at least a few poems wherein he basically admits the location of physical evidence."

I need to swallow, but I'm still trying to look composed for Scardina, so I don't swallow and risk my throat catching as I ask, "You really think Hendee would be stupid enough to write such a poem?"

"If he's a serial killer, it's not a question of stupid," Jonas says. "Serial killers can't help but leave clues, and this guy tends to write confessional poetry to begin with."

I picture myself dressed in something other than a jumpsuit, sitting beside Jonas in a black, bulletproof FBI SUV, headed back to the city with a sunlit Hudson sparkling to my right, the GW Bridge splitting a bright blue sky ahead.

And it's true you no longer know the man like you used to, I think.

And that if you could snap, so could he.

"So what would you need from me?" I ask Jonas. "A signature?"

"For the moment," he says, "an answer in the affirmative would suffice." His eyes appear to be all at once younger, maybe brightened by his FBI ideals—Fidelity, Bravery, Integrity, all that.

And he's assessing me respectfully, like no one has in years, and he's not blinking or flinching. In fact, if anyone's blinking it's me, because, already, despite my decades of friendship with Hendee, I'm tasting freedom, my forehead perspiring, my mind unable to control another vigorous rush of thoughts.

And then I'm doing it, saying two of the many words in my head:

"Okay," I am saying. "Yes."

2

The basement of the Cornelia Café is far less crowded than it was for the readings I'd attend before my twenty-eight minutes. Only nine people are here: an events coordinator named Pearl, the six writers scheduled to read, Jonas, and the supposedly rehabilitated yours truly. Jonas takes a seat on the middle folding chair in the very back row. He's doing his best to present himself as Pat Lynch, literary upstart who drove to NYC from Barstow, CA, in his shabbily refurbished '63 Falcon. Here and now, on this folding chair in the Cornelia, he sits frumpily dressed, tightlipped, arms folded, motionless. True to form as a writer who's just secured representation by an agent who's just been released from prison and whose once-impressive ability to get books published might or might not resurge, he's wearing his hornrims again, holding his chin slightly higher than he would otherwise.

After a quick assessment of the six authors near the stage, I claim the folding chair directly to Jonas's right. For the record, much as I like no longer living in a cage, I still can't believe Hendee could kill. My money says that any taped conversation I'll have with Hendee tonight, if he shows up here as per rumors of poets eavesdropped on by a GS-9 this morning, will prove to the Bureau he's innocent. Precisely what I'll do for the Bureau undercover if it decides he's indeed innocent is something that's not quite clear. One way or another I'll remain in Manhattan, I pray.

The six readers have created two huddles on opposite sides of the stage. On the left and chatting politely enough are the four women, dressed primarily in various shades of gray. On the right, two middle-aged men with apparently nothing to say to each other stand with hands in the pockets of their khakis. Hendee, a second look around assures me, is nowhere.

Then in walks brightness. In fact, from this moment on, my mind will reserve that word—brightness—for this soul only. She's wearing a V-neck white T-shirt and naturally faded jeans tucked into black leather boots with chunky high heels, her onyx-black bob tousled subtly. Her confident black eyes pause on me as she stands behind Jonas and me assessing what she's in for. Clearly, over and above the experience she's had as a woman in her forties, she's nobody's fool, which makes me all the more smitten. No diamond, no jewelry whatsoever. And it's not only her brightness that causes me to want her. It's also the tiny, quick fret that has me certain she's been in some hells too.

Ignore her, I think.

Your soulmate's the Bureau now.

I refocus on maintaining my freedom by facing the two male authors and assessing whether either could be the Success Killer. Relative to Hendee, they're young. They exude tamped-down nervousness. If they sense their chances of commercial success as writers are slim, they're probably clueless about *how* slim. Only an agent with my amount of experience knows that if they were bestselling authors, they wouldn't be here—and that at this point, given the fact that they're in their mid-thirties at the very least, they are in effect wasting their lives.

"Matt?" I hear behind me, and I look over my shoulder to see, at the bottom of the stairs, a robot of a man whose name I can't remember, his arms flat against his sides, his entire being stiffening more the longer he gazes in my direction.

"It's Mitch," he says. "Of *The Pelican Crypt?*"

The face is now familiar even though his thick head of brown hair has been shaved off and he's grown a beard. His last name still escapes me. Then it all comes pounding back: the "novel" that, after I took it on, proved to be so autobiographical it could only be called nonfiction. The compromise he and I made to dub the book "creative memoir." His theory that if the title included words from both *The Pelican Brief* and *Tales from the Crypt*, I'd be able to auction the manuscript overnight— without him deleting dozens of pages that were less engaging still than Scardina's coming-of-age. My failure to sell it to any house whatsoever, the hit my reputation took as a result. The subsequent years of this Mitch guy badmouthing me, or so the rumor mill told me.

I shoot Jonas a look that says, *Suspect?*

But Jonas seems not to care about Mitch in the least—he's enamored of his phone. Hopeful that I'll get Mitch to say something incriminating into the wire, I walk over and shake his hand. In his eyes is sharp disappointment, dashed expectation, or anger, or maybe all three.

"They let you out early," he says.

"They did," I say. "What're you working on, man?"

"A few things, actually."

"I imagine you have representation elsewhere by now."

"I don't. Things of late for me have bottomed out. I mean, writing-wise."

I trust the wire I'm wearing has Jonas hearing this. I wish that in any event he'd slap cuffs on Mitch, who always did creep me out. Mitch grabs my forearm, squeezes it, says, "Let's be in touch," then beelines toward the two male authors standing beside the stage. They shrink back slightly as he approaches, as if he's bad news in their minds. He stops, facing them directly. He's fidgety, apparently uncertain about what to do with his hands—front pockets, back pockets, front pockets, hands on hips.

I glance back at Jonas, who grimaces slightly. I wonder if he's ticked off at me, then notice, standing at the bottom of the staircase, Hendee: haggard, unshaven, and, yes, I have to admit, taking stock of the female writers who are about to read.

Much as Jonas is trying to play it cool, he swallows visibly. As per the instructions he gave me earlier, I place my hand on my chest and scratch it twice. Jonas scratches his left ear, our code to assure me the wire's transmission is fine.

I mosey over to Hendee, who appears to be one with his thoughts.

"Hend!" I say as if delightfully surprised.

He squints at me.

"It's Matt!"

"Hey, hey," he says. "Criminal justice—finally."

We hug, gingerly, and then, just to see how he reacts, I say, "Either that or another violent homicide is in the works?"

He does not flinch. He laughs a hearty, genuine laugh, the laugh one true friend shares with another.

"What are you doing here, man?" he asks. "Weren't you supposed to be—what's the expression?—*on the inside* for a few more years?"

"Early release, baby."

"For good behavior?"

"For excellent behavior."

He smiles, if somewhat nervously.

"You hear what's been going on?" he asks.

"Regarding what?"

"Big houses have been handing out book deals left and right."

"To poets?"

"To novelists. Young ones. In the past few months, three fairly young women with no prior publishing credits hit the jackpot."

And there it is, smack in front me, something I've never seen in Ethan Hendee's eyes: desperation so thick you could almost call it anger.

And why isn't he mentioning that the three women have been murdered? On the other hand, he could be distraught about any number of things, his brother's death included.

Still, this is my chance to get him to talk about the Success Killer's victims, so I ask, "You're telling me you haven't gotten one?"

"A young woman?" he says with a sour smile.

"I meant a book deal, but—"

He looks down at his scuffed cheap shoes. "Nothing either way," he says. "As far as book deals, I've been sending around manuscripts of my better poems on my own. I mean, I hope you don't mind me doing that without your okay."

"Of course I don't mind, Hend. I was behind bars for god's sake. I mean, what were you supposed to do?"

"In any event, no takers. Not even from the tiniest press. It's like it's recently become required even among the *underground* editors to reject me. In fact most of them don't even reject me anymore—they simply don't respond. It's like…well, what's the point in discussing it?"

I nod, not quite sure what to say next. For a few moments, I want to sell a book of his poems more than I want to be an agent for the Bureau. But those moments pass.

"Hey," he says, "I heard about Lauren getting married to Blaine Davis and all. That's pretty wild, man. I mean, I'm sorry to hear it. That is, if it bothers you. Maybe it doesn't by now?"

I shrug as if I never loved Lauren. As if I never rewrote Blaine Davis's breakout book for him from scratch and he never left me for a mega-agency as soon as his big money started flowing in. But my face is heating up again, the roof of my mouth gone dry.

I say, "She finally found her true love, I guess."

And it's just after I say this that Hendee regards me more closely. As if he suspects *me* of something, I'm not sure what. Maybe of lying about how little I care that Lauren remarried? Maybe, if he is the Success Killer, of my being undercover?

"You know, I'm thinking of trying fiction all over again," he says.

I glance over at Jonas, who nods almost imperceptibly.

"Short stories?" I ask nonchalantly.

"A novel," Hendee says. He sets his jaw and clenches it, and it's right then, with him tightlipped like that, that I first truly believe, in my heart, that he could indeed be the Success Killer. I remember "A Quieter Saturday Night," but instead of feeling sorry for him because of his brother's death, I wonder if his brother's death fed into a funk that led him to lash out and kill. I'm confused. I'm upset. I feel faint and wish I could lie on my back on a large bed.

"Excuse me," I hear.

The woman with the tousled bob is beside me, facing me, that black-eyed brightness of hers leaping out toward me.

"Yes?" I manage.

She smiles, kindly. God, does she know what she's doing. Hendee is walking off to take a seat, but I don't care—this is the effect this woman is having.

"Am I correct in assuming, given what I just overheard, that you represent writers of books?" she asks.

"You are."

"Could that include a memoir written by a woman as old as yours truly?"

"It could."

"I'm Em by the way."

"As in Emma?"

"As in Em. My parents, rest their souls, were cool like that."

"My condolences."

"It's fine. They passed on quite a few years back. And a person's gotta move on, right?"

I nod. "I'm Matt," I say. "I'd give you my card, but I just got out of prison."

"So your pal back there wasn't just joking with you."

"He was not."

The brightness in her eyes doesn't fade. If anything, it intensifies. She purses her lips, maybe to gather herself, maybe to fight back a smile. I like her differently than I first liked Lauren. More maturely yet already also somehow more playfully.

She asks, "What did you, uh, *do*?"

"Dispensed with the man who slept with my now ex-wife."

"You mean offed him?"

We share a moment right then of searching each other's faces in that way spouses can. She seems open, emotionally speaking, to my having taken a life, which suggests, to the freelance FBI agent in me, that it's possible she's taken one too.

"Unfortunately," I say.

"When did you get out?" she asks.

"Of the marriage?"

"Of the slammer."

"About four hours ago."

"Which prison was this?"

"The one up in Ossining."

Her eyes, somehow brighter, hold mine. "As in Sing Sing?"

"Yes."

"Guess I should be careful around you."

"Very careful."

"You know there'll be wine upstairs after they read."

"I did *not* know that."

"Free, I heard. And if not, well, you might be able to talk me into buying you a carafe or two."

Jonas and I haven't discussed the Bureau's rules on drinking with potential suspects, but I imagine there must be some. Still, I say, "Sounds ideal. Though I should probably mention: I haven't had a drop in more than four years."

"So you'll be an easy target then."

"For…?"

She cocks her head, gives me a look that says, *Duh.*

An emcee is onstage, introducing himself. Then prattling on about his own publishing credits only to start in on discussing his coming-of-age novel. I remember Scardina's memoir, lean toward Em, and whisper, "Must *every*one?" She continues to face the stage, seemingly intent on absorbing the emcee's every word, but then she not only smiles glowingly, she elbows my ribs—there it is, we have touched.

Better still, with her elbow digging into me, she bends her head toward mine to whisper, "You'll never hear a coming-of-age story out of me."

"Because you're so…" I begin to ask, letting her lean all she wants, and with that she places a finger over my lips and shushes me, causing everyone to look over at us, and then she's off, headed toward the stage, glaring at me as if I alone was the kid in the class causing mischief, nodding at the emcee, then taking a seat directly behind the four women.

That's it, I realize.

Lauren is a gnat on a rearview mirror in the wrecking yard of my unsophisticated past.

I head back toward Jonas, whose eyes pin mine sharply. Doubtless he thinks I should have pressed Hendee to say more. I sit beside him, stare straight ahead, toward the stage. Order myself to think *Fidelity, Bravery, Integrity.*

Still, I can't stop watching the back of Em's bob, waiting for her to move at all, which, of course, she doesn't.

Even her name strikes me as superior to all.

Not Emma, I think.

Just Em.

And those eyes, I think.

And everything else about her: the way she elbowed me, causing the perfect amount of pain, the tickling her whispers aroused, the hiss she made as she shushed me—all of her: killer.

Then I think, Do your job.

The *Success* Killer.

I search the posture of the six seated authors for any sign that might suggest they could do physical harm. They appear completely innocent, pathetically so. How will they, with that fine posture trapped in those crisp neutral-palette clothes, loosen up enough to write something with enough pizazz to induce millions of readers to turn pages?

Jonas, I realize, is typing something into his phone. Then the first author is up, female, redheaded, twenty-something, beauteous. The sentences she imparts are impressively lyrical, suggesting to both the literary agent and the newbie undercover agent in me that she'd never kill anyone. Her writing is also not quite my cup of tea, because the house eds I've worked with have long pressed me for something with plot.

Second comes the tallest of the female readers. Her teeth are crooked, implying a lack of family wealth. Does this mean she feels frustration around privileged writers? If so, is she frustrated enough to kill? I don't know. I give her a chance as both a writer and a suspect. But she goes on to prove to be not much of either. No verve. No edge. Jonas appears to have little interest in her either.

Then the emcee works in one of the men, Thom-something. The several pages he reads detail his experiences as a waiter in Brooklyn. So difficult! And being single in Brooklyn—so lonely! Jonas is still typing, maybe notes about him, but the convict in me does not feel this particular Thom could lure a woman into his apartment—let alone dismember three of them.

The third woman walks to the stage on a cloud of pride. She announces she wants to keep the contents of her "nearly done" novel secret until it's published. She reads "a series of short-shorts" about her mother's hands. She weeps, needs to be escorted offstage. Jonas studies her as she sits but types nothing into his phone.

Then comes the fourth woman, who might be slightly cross-eyed. She speaks with an amount of fear that strikes me as wise. One word and one word only is tattooed across the back of her right hand: *Revise*. She's humble about the fact that a short story of hers, "Fiercely," has, just days ago, been published by *The Paris Review*. I jot her name, Jill Klugman, on page one of the little notepad I bought in the CVS three blocks away, a purchase encouraged by Jonas and paid for by a debit card the Bureau has authorized for me. Jill's *Paris* score, I think, disqualifies her as a suspect—until I realize this recent success doesn't mean she didn't struggle for a decade or more beforehand. Jonas is videotaping her blatantly, a move that makes sense to anyone who's buying his ruse as a literary upstart from Barstow. This calms me because it suggests Jill's replacing Hendee at the top of the Bureau's list. Hendee himself is watching Jill intently, his arms folded, the look on his face sour enough to indicate he wouldn't mind choking her. Jonas doesn't notice this, his focus still on Jill. Em seems enamored of Jill, too, or perhaps only of "Fiercely," which, told in the first person by a female roof deck gardener from Manhattan, narrates the tension between same roof deck gardener and one Vince, a man she's just met and fallen in love with, as they drive to Vermont for her mother's funeral. Vince is about to meet her family, which, unbeknownst to Vince, is into a shit-ton of badassed organized crime. It's a compelling story, indicating Jill Klugman has writing chops as well as authority regarding murder. This, I imagine, is why Jonas keeps training his shiny phone on her.

After Jill finishes, one Cal Fender, a twenty-some-year-old fellow with—talk about teeth—a stunningly white smile, gets up there. Cal's third book of poetry has just been brought out by an Ivy League press. So publishing-wise he's set, leaving him with neither a need for an agent nor a motive to kill, I believe.

I also believe Cal's poems have nothing on Hendee's. In fact, I don't see why Hendee doesn't charge the stage to pummel him.

But Hendee refrains from this. Instead, he stands up, clears his throat, and exits the Cornelia Café.

3

The story I'm supposed to tell about the studio apartment in Chelsea is that I'm subleasing it by the week from an old friend in publishing until I can find a place of my own.

"Mention it casually and no one will doubt you," Jonas says from behind the steering wheel of the idling '63 Falcon. "And, oh, while you were off taking a yaz, I gave that woman the number for the landline up there."

"What woman?"

"Em. The one you were flirting with."

"That wasn't flirting. That was me gathering intel."

"So you agree we should be in touch with her going forward."

"Of course," I say, hoping that only I will be in contact with Em—not Jonas, not anyone else in law enforcement.

"Remember, Mattie, your first loyalty is to the Bureau."

"Why do you say that?"

"Because I can tell you've got it for her."

"Just to be clear: you consider her a suspect?"

"Not really. I'm just reminding you that no way can you tell her—or anyone, no matter how intimate you feel with them—that you're undercover for the Bureau. From her point of view from now on, tonight Pat Lynch was playing wingman for his agent and main man Matt Connell. I mean, that's what authors do for their agents, right? So that's all you and I are when it comes to what you tell her: agent and client."

For a second I think he actually believes I'm representing him.

Then his phone buzzes and he checks its screen. It's a text, apparently, and not a short one. He types in a quick response and, without looking up, says, "Go. Get your sleep. You need to be in good form when we meet with Hendee tomorrow morning for coffee."

"We're meeting Hendee for coffee?"

"That's the plan. This text I just got said a GS-12 tailed him after he left the Cornelia, and he went straight home. So it's still more or less up to us—you, really—to crack his armor."

I nod.

"Use the landline in the apartment to call him."

"Where do you want us to meet him?"

"Nate's Coffee in Brooklyn. He'll figure that's where I like to hang out. Call him ASAP, tell him you want to talk publishing with him there at 10:30. I'll meet you there at 10:00."

I get out of the Falcon, apartment keys in hand. Assess the exterior of my new digs here on Duane, a four-story, red-brick townhouse, all of its lights off. Artsy.

"Talk to you," Jonas says, and he accelerates sharply, causing the passenger side door to slam shut on its own.

An obviously privileged hetero couple strolls past, both looking at their phones. Across the street is a man walking a dog, the dog stopping to pee, the man almost kicking it while slowing down to look at his phone. The city's not what it was, I realize. It's as impressive and able to inspire as ever, but people are barely noticing it.

So this is it, I think. Freedom.

I let myself into my building, a walk-up. My place is #7, on the fourth floor, east-facing, just a room, really. A mere three feet from the foot of the queen bed are two wooden doors that are easily a century old. One's to a closet that's empty save three wire hangers, the other to a bathroom with a toilet whose size strikes me as monstrous compared with the stainless steel one I used in my cell. There's a midcentury modern wooden dresser, in which are several changes of clothes, upon which sits one of those old black rotary jobs. A no-nonsense couch sits between the two east-facing windows, a midnight blue drape hanging over the one beside the bed.

The rotary phone rings. My insides tighten as I grab up the receiver. "Yes?"

"Matt?" a woman's voice asks.

"Em?"

"No. This is Dawn Trinko. With the Bureau? Jonas asked me to remind you that everything on this line is being recorded. And he was worried that maybe you'd forgotten Hendee's phone number, so I can give it to you if you have pen and paper handy."

I quickly pat my pockets for my CVS notebook, to no avail. "I don't, actually."

"There should be a pen and an Algonquin Hotel notepad in an outside pocket of the blazer the Bureau issued you this afternoon."

"I—"

"Left-hand side?"

"Ah," I say. "Got it. Go ahead."

Trinko gives me the number, which I jot, my hand not making numerals as clearly as before my twenty-eight minutes. It's as if I'm four years old again—or ninety.

"Anything else you might need?" she asks.

"No," I say, and she hangs up.

I call Hendee, reach his voicemail, tell him to meet me at Nate's in Brooklyn at 10:30 a.m. I hang up and stand looking at my new four walls. Yes, there are more square feet here than there were in my cell, but not many more. I think ambivalently about heading outside for a walk—I want to feel freer, and being in here doesn't help, though I like it in here. The phone rings. Figuring it's Hendee, I pick up quickly and say, "Hend?"

"Is this Matt?" a woman's voice asks, maybe Trinko, maybe not.

"Who's this?"

"It's damned sure not your warden, buster."

"Is this Em?"

"Of course! Who else would be calling you now? You just got out of the clinker!"

"You'd be surprised."

"So, wait, you're telling me you already have…more accompaniment?"

"No. I'm alone."

"Ah. Good. Do you *like* being alone?"

"You're drunk."

"And you're not?"

"I'd call it more like pleasantly mellowed," I say, and I tell her the address and suggest we meet outside on the stoop.

She doesn't say anything for a stretch of moments I dislike. Her voice—I realize during this silence that I crave the sound of her voice.

Then she says, "I'm in the neighborhood—I'll be there," and hangs up.

I unbutton the white button-down the Bureau issued me, yank the wire and the tape off my chest, hide both beneath the mattress. It occurs to me the Bureau heard me do this through the wire itself, but I am, I remind myself, an adult just out of prison, and at some point in anyone's life, true physical love is necessary. And if Em is indeed the Success Killer, how better to gain her trust—so I can prove that she is—than to spend the night with her?

I brush my teeth with the Bureau's toothbrush and toothpaste. Using the small bathroom faucet, I wash my face, careful to keep my hair dry. Button the shirt except for the top button—I know not to look like I'm trying.

I head out. On Duane I watch more people walk past while looking at their phones. They do not see me, or the rat that skitters across the sidewalk to my left. But while I wait, I notice only that one rat: while I was doing time, the city has cleaned up.

Then I hear, "Hey."

Even with the moon hidden behind clouds, she looks brighter than sunshine at noon on the Fourth of July.

"Hey."

"Shall we?" she says, pointing at the door.

I lead us up the stoop to it, open it. She steps up ahead of me and glides in. The only reason I'm not falling for her is I already have. We say nothing as we climb the stairs. She leans against me for a priceless moment as I unlock the apartment door. Once we're inside and she's closed and locked the door behind us, she clears her throat softly and says, "Lovely."

I step over to the window past the foot of the bed. Outside I see the moonlit, painted-silver roof of the building just east. On it is a sawhorse, some white five-gallon buckets, power cords.

I feel her beside me, studying the roof too.

"Tell me what you want me to know," she says.

"About what?"

"About you-know what."

I nod. I'm ecstatic, merely standing this close to her. Happiness, I think. This is what it always was, I think.

I say, "It all went down in twenty-eight minutes."

"From when you caught her?"

"From when I found out about it."

"How did you find out?"

"A client told me. While he and I were having lunch."

"And then twenty-eight minutes later, the guy who was bopping your wife was dead."

"*Bopping.*"

"Yeah. When it's adultery, I prefer to deem it mere bopping."

"You've been through something similar?"

She says nothing. She's still staring at the silver roof. Placid as can be. And gorgeous.

Then, with confidence, she says, "Yes."

"Did you want to tell me about that?"

"Not now. For now, I like hearing us talk about you."

"Okay. So, yes, whatever we might decide to call it, you're right—twenty-eight minutes later, the guy who was bopping my wife was dead."

She continues to stare out. Says, "Well, there's a certain justice to that."

"That's what I've often told myself."

"While lying awake in your cell."

"Yes."

"Anyhow, that's all in the past, right?"

"I don't know. Is it?"

"Isn't it?"

"In my mind it is—that is, as much as a homicide can be. I don't know about in yours."

"My mind can be a trip," she says.

"What does that mean?"

"It means I'm finding you perfectly to my liking, but given some of the things I've been through, my mind might someday prove to go off on a rail of its own."

Meaning she's the Success Killer? I think, and I'm about to ask her directly if she's ever killed anyone, but her reticence convinces me she needs more assurance that we're kindred spirits.

"Maybe you're more like me than I realized?" I say.

"How so?"

"When I learn I've been deceived about something horrible, I get bombarded by all kinds of thoughts, and the thoughts run off and go into this sort of swirl in my mind, and sometimes some of the thoughts are...homicidal."

"You're saying this—this kind of bombardment—happened when your client told you about the guy bopping your ex?"

"Yes. It was the first thing that happened in my twenty-eight minutes. My mind just sort of...took off uncontrollably."

"Uh-huh."

"And I guess I'm thinking you should probably know this sometimes still happens."

"The rush of thoughts?"

"Yes."

"It happens whenever you think about your ex?"

"Whenever I've been deceived."

"About something horrible."

"Yes."

"So you're saying you don't react well to being hood-winked—about horrible things."

"Yes. You could put it that way."

We continue to stand still. I want her to lean on me again. Or at least speak.

Which, finally, she does:

"Ferrari brain."

"Pardon?"

"I have it too. Your mind's been trained to problem-solve on the fly for so long—probably because of your shitty childhood—that it responds to bad news with a rush of thoughts about worst-case scenarios, not to mention a zillion things you can do to protect yourself. And then, well, sometimes there can be so many thoughts so fast, the sheer bulk of them can overwhelm you."

"Sounds about right. You make this theory up?"

"Nope."

"Learned it in therapy?"

"Actually, I heard about it on a podcast."

"That's funny."

"Not when you yourself have Ferrari brain."

"Which you know you have because…you've been deceived about being cheated on and committed homicide too?"

"Deceived about being cheated on, yes. Homicide no. Though I will admit to thinking about homicide."

"After your husband cheated on you."

"After an ex did. I haven't quite done the marriage thing yet, Matt. Came close, but…not to sound cheesy, but my hope's always been to try that only once."

We both go still, considering this.

I say, "Admirable, as hopes go."

"Maybe. Though if you're unpartnered, life can sometimes start to feel as if it's getting very long, you know what I mean?"

Unpartnered? I think. How can a woman this sexy be unpartnered?

Must've done *something* bad, I think.

"Of course I know," I say.

"Oh. Right. What with being in prison and all. Sorry—I can be such a goof sometimes."

"Anyway, for you," I ask, "the acceleration of thoughts happens when you're envious?"

"'Jealous' would be the precise word there, no? But come to think of it, it has also happened to me when I've been envious."

Meaning what? I think. She's envied other writers their successes—and killed the three women?

No.

She's too hot, too calm.

Too smart, too beautiful, too altogether bright.

"Ferrari brain is a medical term?" I ask.

"No. That's just what the guest on the podcast called it. I refuse to consider it a disorder. If you ask me, it's an indicator of genius."

I smile. If she doesn't have all of my heart, she has all of my body, spirit, and mind—because when it comes to the way my mind works, she knows exactly how to talk.

"So are we done sharing deep, dark secrets for the night?" she asks.

"I don't know. You decide."

"I think we've done an impressive amount of that kind of sharing."

"I think I'd say I agree."

She takes my hand and leads me to the bed. Kisses the back of my wrist, nibbles it before she lets me go. Stands on her toes to kiss a side of my neck, then my earlobe, which she bites just hard enough to send pain and maybe a little panic down my neck.

"You do realize," I say, "that it's been more than four years."

She pushes me back until I'm sitting on the bed, facing her. Wedges herself between my knees, eases herself closer to me. She's still standing. She places her hands on my shoulders and squeezes them, out of her own curiosity, it seems.

"You can squeeze me, too, you know," she says.

"I know."

"You don't want to?"

"I want to absolutely. I guess I was just using the old, you know, delay trick."

She takes hold of one of my thighs with both of her hands, sits on the other.

"This okay?" she asks.

"It's phenomenal."

"You still like me?"

"Yes."

"You're better at the delay game than anyone I've ever been with."

I nod.

I ask, "Was that use of the word 'anyone' your way of saying there've been women?"

"How astute of you."

"Not really."

"Don't be modest. Let me admire you. It'll pay off for you—trust me."

"You think?"

"I know."

She slings an arm around my neck, tugs me toward her a little. "And how about you? Maybe there was some handsome young nightshift guard in the clinker?"

I grin and roll my eyes. "No."

"So you relied upon yourself, huh."

"No."

"*No?*"

"That's correct."

"But how can that be?"

"Because anything along those lines was simply not possible for me in there."

"You're telling me you never…once…since your arrest?"

"That's correct also."

She tugs me toward her again. "Damn. Looks like I'm about to be on the receiving end of quite a bit of restraint."

"It wasn't restraint. It was like everything in that realm was shut off."

"Because you were ashamed? Because you needed to prove you were good? I don't get it. I—"

"I guess I was…I don't know exactly. I guess I was still upset?"

"But you did strangle to death the offending party, right?"

I nod.

She kisses my forehead. "What was his name again, Considine?"

"I called him Consee. We'd been fairly close pals beforehand. How did you know his name—and that I strangled him?"

"Google."

"When did you google it, on your way here?"

"While that doofus from Brooklyn was reading."

"Well, Google got the how part right."

"You mean about strangulation being your…modus?"

"Yes."

"Can I ask you something personal?"

"Of course."

"Did you still feel angry after you killed this…Consee?"

I need to look off to remember well enough to answer truthfully.

With my eyes fixed on the door, I say, "Yes."

"Angry at your wife, or at Consee's departed soul?"

I'm not sure how to answer this. Because for a good while when I was first doing time, I still loved Lauren, or believed I did. It's tough to say now, as I enjoy the sensations of Em sitting on my lap, if I felt love or anger toward Lauren for the year that followed my twenty-eight minutes.

"Probably both," I say.

"What about now? You feel ready to put her out of your life for good?"

"She's already out."

"But she put herself out. Now *you* can put *her* out."

Then we are kissing. There's something about the candor

of what she just said that has me on edge. We keep kissing while we are lying on the bed, all of our clothes still on, she on me, not shy about pressing herself against me, but I'm not responding, not in the least.

"Or maybe I can't," I say.

"Don't be silly," she says, and she bites my earlobe, pressing herself harder against me, but my mind's off and into memories of my twenty-eight minutes, concern that I need more rehab than I've had, and speculation about whether Em or Hendee is the Success Killer.

"Maybe," I say, now worried about how I might not see her again because I can't get it up, which accelerates the whirl of thoughts in me, bringing to mind a train of words that have haunted me since my twenty-eight minutes: *loser, arrested, defendant, guilty, manslaughter, convicted, inmate.*

"Maybe you think I'm too aggressive?" she whispers into my ear.

"No. This—us together like this—is exactly what I wanted. It's my mind. I mean, I can't stop it."

"Ferrari brain," she says.

"But how is that an excuse for *this?*"

"Because I've had this happen too."

"You mean inability to…mess around?"

She laughs. Goddamn, I think. She gets me. She says, "Don't worry, Mr. Matt. Just remember something you yourself have known for at least four years: none of these rushes of thoughts lasts forever."

"That's true."

"So if you're anything at all like me, you and I are going to team up to do some serious damage."

"Meaning precisely what?" I ask.

She kisses my nose, my forehead, my mouth. "Meaning precisely what it implies: if not tonight, or tomorrow, or the day after that, we're going to have a grand time."

4

Until the Success Killer is caught, Jonas will be living in Bed-Stuy, a few A-and-C-line stops away from Nate's Coffee. Not the section of Bed-Stuy that's already been gentrified. The section that's still gritty—where any writer from Barstow lacking a book deal would live in order to afford rent. When it comes to creating personas for its undercover personnel, the FBI doesn't mess around.

Nate's Coffee, as Jonas's cover suggests, is where Jonas goes every morning in search of fellow artistes. Yes, he supposedly has me as his literary agent, but—well, in Brooklyn authors tend to flock with other authors, and this flocking happens at Nate's.

Anyway I walk into the place.

"Jonas."

"Matt."

I give the place the once-over. Of the dozen or so people, half appear to be aspiring writers. On the back of Jonas's chair hangs a backpack. On the table in front of his coffee rest three pens and a college-ruled notebook. He jots as I sit. Careful not to nick the coffee he's ordered for me, he spins the notebook so I can read:

You call Hendee?

I nod.

Again, he writes:

Did Em visit?

He shoves one of the other pens toward me, making it clear we should say nothing aloud.

Yes, I write.

Why did you take off the wire?

Because I didn't want her to feel it.

So things got physical?

No.

Good.

I assess his face. He appears dead-serious.

He adds, *Keep it that way.*

You mean no fooling around?

No. In fact, involvement fine. Whatever it takes to get her confidence. Just don't let her know you're UC—or it's back to Sing Sing.

UC?

Undercover.

I nod and look off, studying the patrons, most of them facing their laptops.

As I glance back, he sips. Apparently he takes neither milk nor cream, and for this morning, I decide, I won't either.

I turn the page in his notebook, jot at the top of a fresh page: *What about Mitchell Parker?*

What about him?

Is he on our radar?

Why would he be?

Failed writer, just like Hendee. Struck me as nervous last night.

He shrugs. Between the notebook's last page and back cover he finds a piece of paper he removes. Another xeroxed poem that was published in a small mag and written by Hendee.

"Thought you might like to read this," he says loud enough for the wannabe writers around us to hear. "A Hendee poem," he says even more loudly.

I take the poem and read it carefully:

Muse

she'd heard I had
an agent & asked me to dinner
& I ate the dinner with
her & she'd heard I'd lived
in only one room & asked
if she could
see it & I said sure

& in the one room
she stepped to my desk
read a letter
from the agent
removed her blouse
jeans
bra
sat on the bed & said
"get over here"

through most of it I felt used
& when she was done
she stood upright
dressed facing away from me

then turned
kissed my mouth
& without even saying good-bye
left forever

that agent never selling
a word of mine

the woman herself
going on to author
a bestselling book

while here I continue
to sit alone

doing little
more than typing

"Can I read that?" asks a high-pitched voice behind me.

I turn. She's stopped there, about a foot directly behind me, with a venti of something magic-markered JENN. Well-scrubbed, apparently from good money, smug expression.

"No," Jonas says to her. "This is my agent, uh, *Jennifer,* and

I worked my butt off to sign with him. So if you'd like to talk with him, I'd suggest you query him like I did."

"Are you Matt Connell?" the woman asks me.

"I am."

"The agent who just got out of prison?"

"Yes."

She drops her eyes to check out my Bureau-issued khakis and brown wingtips.

"Where you were serving time because you murdered that philandering novelist?"

"It was manslaughter, but yes."

"Well, I happen to think he deserved what you did to him. Can I get a pic with you?"

"Maybe later?" I say. "I need to talk branding with this guy. By the way, look for his work—he's got a great novel I'm about sell. His name is Pat Lynch."

She nods and says, "J.T. Hones. Look for me in your inbox?"

"Sure."

She douses Jonas with an envious glare, returns to her table. *Suspect?* I jot on Jonas's notebook, but he already has his phone out, its video camera on.

Recorded the whole conv, he writes.

In any case, I'd say this Jenn is buying Jonas's status as an upstart Bed-Stuy novelist who I've recently taken on as a client—she believes all of it. And now her thumbs are tapping her phone, maybe posting something: Pat Lynch's fame might already be blossoming.

"So what do you think?" he asks me.

"Of her?"

"Of Hendee's poem."

"Hadn't seen it before."

He turns the page in his notebook, scrawls:

The issue just came out a few days ago. Which means H probably wrote the poem within the past year or so.

Not necessarily, I think, but I don't want to quibble right now.

He writes:

Trinko's take is he's significantly ticked off at you.

I jot, *So?*

So if he's TSK...

TSK?

The Success Killer.

I raise my eyebrows. *Then what?*

THEN YOU COULD BE THE NEXT VICTIM.

But I'm not female.

True.

Plus: Really? Puny Ethan Hendee, kick MY ass???

He takes back "The Muse," folds it, stuffs it into an inside pocket of his sharkskin blazer, which, if you ask me, looks a bit too much like mine.

Then we sit drinking our coffees, pretending to harbor literary thoughts.

Then he unzips his backpack, removes from it a phone as large and slick as his, hands it over.

"What's this for?" I ask.

"It's yours."

"No-no-no, man. Not a smartphone person. Never was. Before my arrest I was the only agent in Manhattan who was landline-only. It not only distinguished me, it decreased my supply—which, as it turned out, increased demand."

Jonas sips coffee, starts a new page:

Standard issue if you want to work with the Bureau, bruh. Harnischfeger says so.

I jot:

Who's Harnischfeger?

Our boss for this case.

He leans across the table to whisper quietly:

"This way if you run into someone when you're not wired up, we can still hear them. You just hit record and keep your blazer unbuttoned and this thing'll record any conversation you have. And if, say, Hendee goes off on you with a hatchet and mistakenly leaves you for dead, there's a help button you can push with a tracking device for us. And of course you can take extremely hi-res photos and vids—and let's face it: you're in the business of finding *evidence.*"

He leans closer now, intent.

"It's the same kind I use, and I love it," he says.

And it occurs to me that maybe he's never had a real friend. Obviously he's never had a literary agent in real life, but as I see things now, what the real Paul Jonas needs is a pal.

"If nothing else," he mutters, sitting back. "If nothing else take it because Em has the number to it too."

The phone, of course, is dazzling. I snatch it off the tabletop and slide it into my blazer's inside pocket.

Jonas nods, picks up his own phone, begins a series of text conversations with headquarters. This is the brunt of under-cover work, apparently: texting. Not all that dissimilar from what I did for years via email to sell manuscripts. The difference being Jonas doesn't stop to entertain meandering thoughts about interpersonal feelings; his intent thumbs hammer his shiny screen rapid-fire. Confident and inspired, he has no time for his coffee, let alone a biscotti. And as I sit sipping and hoping Em will call, I want to be such a man—that is, if that's possible without sending Hendee to prison.

Wouldn't it be great? I realize. To work for the rest of my life with no-bullshit colleagues like him, a whole network of people bent on fidelity, bravery, and integrity?

At some point he aims his horse face my way and, squinting, asks, "Come up with a way to get Hendee to open up with us?"

"I think so," I say. "You and he, the supercool young writer from Cali and the veteran poet from New York: co-authors. Big book. Major publisher, if I can swing it. Poems by him and maybe some prose poems from you, an interview of both of you by someone like Kasha Kackimo. We'll call the interview 'a conversation.' And that'll be the title of the book: *A Conversation.*"

"Who's Kasha Kackimo?"

"Goddess in poetry."

"Does Hendee like her?"

"Let's hope. To be honest, I'd need her name on the cover of the book in order to get a big publisher to bite, and I'm fairly certain Hendee knows this."

"Okay. Sounds like a winner."

Jonas returns to his texting. I wonder whether this idea of mine for a book could actually sell. And if it could, who'd write the prose poems supposedly from Jonas?

Then Hendee is there. Just inside the doorway. Jonas sets down his phone, which I figure is recording. In the event it's not, I take mine out and place it on the table, searching the icons on it for one that says record, unable to find anything of the sort. Jonas turns the page on his notebook and pretends to free-write. Hendee's holding the door open, hesitant. He's eyeing all of Nate's patrons, including Jenn, who notices him, picks up her phone, apparently to text or post something about him.

"Hend!" I call.

He sees me. I wave him over. He notices Jonas, smiles meekly at me as he approaches. I remember Blaine Davis telling me about Consee and Lauren, then brush away the thought to say, "Have a seat, man."

"Pat Lynch," Jonas says with a casual nod at Hendee. "A pleasure."

They shake with some apparent goodwill. They do not seem to be oil and water from the start. I've seen writers despise each other from moment one, others whose mutual respect collapses quickly into curse-fests. I remember it was a writer, Consee, who ruined my life.

I get right to it about *A Conversation*. Hendee listens while Jonas acts as if he's only now hearing about the idea.

Altogether, Hendee seems unimpressed. The first thing he says is, "Why a conversation?"

Then Jonas engages him in small talk about the lit-mag game. For someone who never wrote poetry in real life, Jonas knows a hell of a lot about who edits which mags—no doubt the guy's done significant homework. He even goes on at length about the seventy-seven straight rejections he supposedly once had. Hendee laughs along empathetically, if with some reticence.

Then Hendee says, "Matt, I was wondering if you could stop by my place soon? About some…you know, private stuff?"

"Sure," I say, though I figure Jonas probably wants to wire me up first. "How 'bout this afternoon?" I ask.

"I was thinking ASAP," Hendee says. "It's fairly urgent personal stuff."

"Of course," I say. "Let me wrap up this other thing with Jonas, then I'll cab over to your place—would forty-five minutes be okay?"

"You know, just forget it," he says. "I didn't mean to keep you from whatever you got going on with this guy."

So there it is: raw envy on Hendee's part. Bursting out so forcefully it sounded like a motive to kill.

"Hend," I say. "Relax. You are the man, and we all know it. In fact, let's you and I go over to your place right now. Pat and I—Pat, we can talk over drinks tonight, right?"

Jonas nods and says, "As long as you deliver the deal."

I stand. Hendee's expression has gone somber—clearly he needs to spill his guts about something, and as I follow him toward the door, I believe I'm about to hang out alone with the Success Killer.

"Uh, Matt?" Jonas calls loudly when I reach the door.

I turn away from Hendee, who's already walking out and about to cross Hicks Street. I let my eyes ask Jonas, *What else am I supposed to do?*

"Your phone?" he calls with a manufactured grin.

He holds up my phone, and I jog back over to him, see him press an icon on its screen, and take it.

"You're a successful agent!" he shouts as I again head off. "How can you forget your *phone?*"

5

Forty-seven Mott," is all Hendee says during our cab ride to Chinatown. He still lives where I last knew him to live, in the basement of a decrepit, skinny building whose first floor and basement were once a mani-pedi-massage spa. Flanking this spa to the south has long been a tiny shop that still sells knockoff watches and purses and cheap sunglasses in a rainbow of colors. To the north is a newer but tinier place where a locksmith is also still in business, though clearly that locksmith deals in far more than the deadbolts he installs and the brass keys he cuts. Rent in Chinatown is cheap, but not that cheap.

Unless you're in Hendee's situation. That is, unless you live in the basement level of a cramped, permanently closed mani-pedi-massage joint whose aluminum window guard has been pulled down and padlocked for good so long ago its graffiti has been graffitied upon for years.

Meaning no sunlight can reach the floor above you, let alone where you live. Also meaning that, to take your agent to your living quarters, you need to escort him through the narrow alleyway *behind* your building, unlock the horizontal storm door of sorts that leads to the rear of the basement, raise that door so you and he can descend concrete stairs probably once used to accept deliveries of illegally imported whatnot.

And as soon as I follow Hendee past the four large black rat hotels on those concrete stairs, I am sweating. The basement is eighty degrees at least. Why Hendee's body hasn't shut down due to heat exhaustion eludes me. How does the guy sleep? No wonder he has trouble with women.

He leads me down a dim passageway fronting the cheap drywalling job that created four former massage rooms to our right. The first two we pass are secured by thick padlocks. Storage units, by the looks of them, and why couldn't a freezer or two be in one or two of them? I smell a mild, rubbery stink. I stop in my tracks for fear of encountering more evidence, pretend to cough a few times as my excuse for not following him closely. As he hangs a right into the unit closest to the front of the building, I double-check my phone to make sure it's still recording (I found the record icon in the cab on the way here), return it to my pocket, proceed ahead.

Hendee has managed to live here without working a traditional job because way, way back, in those years when I used to tell him I'd have a book contract for him within days, a trust from a dead uncle afforded him thirty years to do nothing but write in Manhattan—that is, if he'd scrimp for all thirty.

And here we are, twenty-eight and a half years after that trust was seeded, in this skinny hell in Chinatown. Illuminated only by a few LED book lights clamped to gouged-out electrical sockets overhead.

"LEDs a hip touch," I say, still just outside of the cramped unit he's standing in, which is smaller than the cell I lived in upstate.

"Cheaper that way," he says as I step inside. The floor beneath my feet is carpeted by drafts of poems that may or may not go on to be published. A desk has a pair of downward-aimed LED book lights clipped overhead. There's a five-foot-high doorway sawed out from the plasterboard wall to our right, to allow passage into the next unit over, where he keeps a cot as well as his laptop and printer, both smudged here and there with something red. Probably ink, I tell myself, but who knows?

The floor in this second room is even more thickly covered by drafts of his unpublished verse.

"You have a second unit now!" is all I can think to say.

"I do."

We both stand motionless, looking around. Is this how he does it? I wonder. One minute you're getting the grand tour, and the next he attacks?

"Still no fridge, huh," I say.

And right then, I must admit, Hendee appears not only to dislike this question, but also to mistrust me for asking it.

"Still hate to cook, Matt," he says.

That's the irony in Hendee's artsy poverty: The man has never made a meal in New York. Every morsel he's swallowed since he moved from Pennsylvania three decades ago has been from any of four restaurants in Chinatown, all Chinese. Sometimes, to try to make the proceeds of his trust fund last longer, he's bought a bagful of fried dumplings for a quarter from a guy about to toss the night's abandoned phone-in orders in the dumpster behind one of those restaurants. I remember once tagging along when he bought me dinner like that. "As long as it doesn't go *in* the dumpster," he said, "why not?"

"So what was it you wanted to discuss?" I ask now, speaking up louder with my new Bureau phone in mind. For a moment I despise this about being an agent, any kind of agent: being caught between party one's and party two's needs with no one giving a damn about party three—yourself.

"It's more like I wanted to give you something," Hendee says. "And then say goodbye."

"What? What do you mean goodbye?"

"I'm leaving the country, Matt."

Mother of God, I think. He killed the three women. I lean slightly closer to him—I want the phone in my pocket to transmit as clearly as possible.

"You okay?" he asks.

"Sure. Why?"

"You're, like, listing."

"I'm fine. I was just…you know, eager to hear what you had to say. I mean, you're leaving, man—I just got out and you're *leaving?*"

"I just need to," he says.

"For what? A little vacation?"

"For good."

My eyes rove in search of anything he might have used as a weapon. I notice a large stapler. I see beside the stained-red printer a paring knife, albeit beside a brown apple core. "To where?" I ask. "Hend, this is all very surprising."

"Mexico."

"You mean, in one of those towns just over the border, or..."

"San Miguel de Allende."

"With all the artistes?"

He nods.

"But why, Hend? I thought you didn't really gel with other... you know, creative people."

"I don't. But that place is pretty much my only option, cost-wise. And I gotta get out of this country, Matt. My flight's in five hours, and that's that."

"Why? You've been writing *stellar* poems here! I mean, Hend, I realize you still haven't exactly grabbed the brass ring, but you *are* the unofficial poet laureate of the United States! You've had more poems published than anyone alive in the past fifty years, and your poems...every single one of them has *soul*!"

"Soul schmoul, Matt. It's time for you also to get real. It's all about ugly polemics, man—no one gives a shit about soul. It's about attacking and defeating and...killing, actually. And I simply can't handle the attacks anymore. They don't sit well with me; I don't react very well to being hated. Not well at all, if you must know the truth. Anyway, do you realize how many times I've heard that bullshit speech of yours?"

Jonas? I think. *Are you getting this?*

"It's not a speech, Hend," I say. "And it's certainly not bull-shit. It's just a straightforward pep talk. The same one I gave you the day before you submitted that poem that landed in *The New Yorker*. And now you have this book coming up."

"What book?"

"*A Conversation!*"

"That book's not gonna be mine."

"Okay, I realize it's kind of only half yours, but you're the headliner—"

"A third."

"Pardon?"

"It would be only a third mine. That's no actual book for me."

"Sure it is."

"There'll be that Lynch guy's work in it—and, frankly, Matt, I have no idea why you'd want to pair me with a wannabe like him. And there's also going to be Kasha's self-serving lead-up to each question she asks. On top of which there's no way she won't finagle at least a dozen of her poems into a prologue she'll insist on. Which means I'd be lucky to land maybe a third of the page count—that's like being in an anthology. I mean, come on, Matt, don't you realize that no one buys anthologies anymore?"

Hendee's eyes are daggers.

"Plus, to be honest?" he says. "I really don't like Lynch. I've seen posers before, but...*Christ*. Seriously, who *is* he? I haven't seen his name in the mags, not even once, and just like that you're taking him on?"

I go tongue-tied. I've never seen Hendee this livid. His left hand is within two feet of the paring knife, so I take tiny glances in that direction while keeping my mouth shut.

And then, possibly worse, instead of venting more, he falls silent. A dead-serious look remains on his face. If his hand makes as much as a twitch toward that knife, I'll tackle him.

His eyes drop, intent on a drafted poem on the floor.

"Okay, Hend," I say. "Okay. I'm gonna get you a deal of your own. Just you, no Lynch, no Kasha. The whole book nothing but your poems. I'm gonna do it."

"How? You're a goddamned *ex-con*! You're probably even more washed up than I am!"

"Same way I was gonna get this *Conversation* deal. I'll go to the very same publisher and insist on a two-book deal, the first book being a collection of your poems and yours only. I can do this, Hend. You're right about me being an ex-con, but apparently a few acquiring eds are getting a kick out of knowing me because I'm tight with drug dealers and hitmen and so on—they think I can help them sign some marketable memoirs."

Hendee's expression softens some.

Then he says, "Anyway I'm going to Mexico."

"But, Hend—"

"And I want you to have this."

He snatches up the draft he was looking at. Reads it silently, hisses out an angry breath, shakes his head, tosses that draft back down. Looks around more, checks past the doorway into the room with the desk. Steps into that room and grunts as he reaches down, I can't see what for. Then I see, in his hand, another printed-out draft.

He reads this as if proofing it down to the spacing between words. Reaches toward the paring knife only to take a flash drive off that corner of the desk. Hands me the flash drive, then the draft.

"I doubt you'll ever sell a book of mine, Matt," he says. "But if you do someday, the poems on this flash drive are my best. I don't care what any editor says—if a big house wants to put out a book of Ethan Hendee's best poems, these are it."

"Okay," I say, and I slip the flash drive into an outside pocket of my blazer.

"And thank you," he says. "For your effort over the years. You tried, brother. I know I whined now and then about you not going to bat for me, but from today on, be assured I appreciated you and always will. So, again: thank you."

"You're welcome," I say, but my mind's onto telling me that he probably killed the three women, that there might be evidence to this effect in the poems on the flash drive, that he probably won't make it to Mexico—if I do what the Bureau expects me to.

"So, well, that's it," he says, and he heads back down the hot, dim hallway. I consider asking him point-blank if he's the Success Killer but again smell the mild stink, then decide to keep my mouth shut and follow him.

When we're outside, in the narrow alleyway, I realize the

poem he gave me is still in my hand. I tap him on the shoulder, raise the poem slightly, and say, "What's this?"

"My best ever," he says. "If you do ever sell a manuscript of mine—and maybe all it'll take for that to happen is for me to leave this frickin' country—make sure that one ends up being in it, preferably at the very end. I didn't have time to save it onto that flash drive, but please make sure it gets in."

"You got it," I say. I step toward him for a goodbye hug, but he raises a hand to stop me.

"Can't," he says. "I'm wigging out enough."

His face reflects anger, fatigue, impatience, frustration, sadness, wonderment, and, maybe more than any of these, inroads toward relief.

We exchange nods, and I'm off.

When I'm out on Mott, facing uptown, I stop to read the poem in my hand as pedestrians stream past me in both directions.

Hope

"it's a shockingly
nice-looking parakeet"
the whore said
& the old man
sat up & said

"that's what I used to think"

"before your wife cheated on you?"
she asked

& he cleared his throat
swallowed hard &—quietly—said "yes"

she stepped to the window
unlocked it
raised it 2 inches

the old man didn't move so she
raised it 6 more

the parakeet shivered
blinked
let its feathers settle
hopped onto the gritty
side of the sill

she returned to the old man
sat beside him again

her hand found his
titanium knee

"you sure we should
let that thing
sit out there?" he asked

the parakeet dropped itself
to the dirt
beside the dry-rotted siding &
the bird-crap-stained lot

it was out of sight until the old man
saw it hopping again
& again
then standing out there
in the dark like a small
faded statue of St. Jude

nighttime was out there

Mexico was out there

no one would see shit until sunrise

"thing's gonna get
pecked to hell by those
crows in that olive tree"
the old man said

the whore stood
walked to the window
& looked out at
the only world she knew

"those crows" she said carefully
"are gone"

I remain standing still in the flow of people, to let this one sink in. Did Hendee intend the old man to represent me, since the old man's been cheated on?

No, I think. He doesn't care that much about you—you never sold a book for him. The old man symbolizes him.

I fold the poem, slide it into a front pocket of my khakis. Despite its quirkiness and depth, I think, it'll never make its way into a book, not even if I'd kiss up to every contact I know. Too in-your-face, I think. Too gritty.

My FBI phone rings. I remove it and tap the green icon that's shaped like a phone.

"Jonas?"

"Matt?" a woman's voice says.

"Dawn?"

"*Dawn*? This is Em."

"Em!" I say, trying to sound playful, very likely failing.

"If you're busy, my friend, just say boo and I'm gone."

Somehow, even those words from her lift my spirit. "It's fine," I say. "If I get a click-in I'll need to go, but I'm glad you called."

"Glad you're glad. How you doing otherwise?"

"I'm…adjusting."

"To freedom?"

"I guess we could call it that."

The line goes quiet so long I'm sure we're cut off.

Then she says, "Can I ask another question?"

"Sure."

"Is Lauren…is she still the one?"

I don't know how to answer this. I am walking again, though.

"Let's put it this way," I say. "She *was* the one."

I hear a click, maybe a call-waiting.

"Is that on your end?" she asks.

"If so, talk soon," I say, and I tap her away, and then Jonas is in my ear, miffed as he asks, "What's going on with Hendee?"

"Just left his place," I say. "I assume you heard what he said about his plans."

"No. I did not."

"What?" I say, incredulous. I'm on Canal now, headed west.

"Don't mess with me, Matt," Jonas says. "You didn't transmit and we both know it."

"What do you mean? It was recording!"

"All we heard were bits and pieces, and then you cut off. So—catch me up."

I realize I could keep secret Hendee's plans to flee. I might have more power now than I've ever had.

"Do you want me to tell you right away?" I ask. "Because it's huge, and I'm right out here walking on Canal, with people all around me."

"Is he following you?"

I look over my shoulder, check both sides of Canal.

"I don't see him," I say.

"Did you look in the cabs?"

"Hang on."

I check the cabs and cars behind me best I can. Traffic is more or less stopped.

"I think we're okay," I say.

"So what's the word?"

"He's leaving for Mexico in a few hours."

"For good?"

"That's what he told me."

"Did you see a freezer?"

"No. But there were two padlocked units where a couple of freezers could've been hidden."

"Anything else?"

I can't get my mind to accept completely that Hendee killed anyone, but I'm saying, as if concerned, "He has a knife, Jonas. A small one, but still."

"Did you see any blood?"

"I saw smears of red, but those might have been ink. Though I have to tell you: in the hallway outside the padlocked doors, there was a weird smell."

"Like rotten ground beef?"

"What I smelled was…kind of rubbery."

"Okay, man. This is all huge. So, okay. So while I call this in to Harnischfeger, get your ass over to the main library on Forty-First and Fifth. That's our headquarters—I mean yours and mine for this case. I'll meet you on those white marble stairs to the main entrance. Harnischfeger'll be there with an affidavit for you to sign. Meanwhile, brother, watch your ass. And oh: Excellent work, Matt. Crackerjack. Now get over to Forty-First ASAP."

6

As I approach Jonas on those hallowed white stairs, it occurs to me that my affiliation with the FBI might be over far sooner than I thought. I don't want it to be over. I want employment from the Bureau, with a salary and benefits and all that. I have little faith in my long-term future as an agent of the sort I was before my arrest, that is, a literary agent: my having represented a serial killer will not fly well in major house conference rooms, especially since on top of that, there's my twenty-eight minutes.

With this in mind, I follow Jonas up the stairs toward the library's monstrous entrance. We have yet to speak, and the pace of Jonas's stride says we won't until we're in the presence of Harnischfeger.

We enter the building to the smell of books. My breathing goes shallow. Fondness for Hendee keeps colliding with the notion that he could kill. Though something wasn't right with him, I keep telling myself. I'm walking briskly, following Jonas down a wide corridor. The Bureau's correct, I think. Hendee couldn't handle never having grabbed the brass ring.

Jonas steps into a maintenance elevator we take down. After it stops, I follow him through a labyrinth of gray hallways. He removes his phone, swipes it, thumbs it. A door in front of us opens.

"Harnischfeger," Jonas says.

"Jonas."

Harnischfeger is hunched yet muscle-bound. He might be as old as sixty. His hair's either dyed expertly or as extraordinarily black for his age as mine is white.

"Good to meet you, Connell," he says.

"Same," I say, and we shake, his grip assuring me he could kick my ass with one quick uppercut.

"We have an affidavit here saying Hendee told you directly, face to face, that he plans to leave the country within hours, and that there are two padlocked rooms in his domicile."

"How'd you get this typed up and over here so fast?"

"We're the FBI, Matt."

"Right."

"Will you sign it?"

"Do I have a choice?"

"Absolutely. If one word in there isn't true…"

"What's this part here about Hendee 'appearing fidgety and nervous, as if he very well was planning to leave the country for Mexico because he'd committed a crime'?"

"We went out on a limb there," Harnischfeger says. "If you prefer, we can tweak it out."

Jonas, I notice, is watching me eagerly. He wants an arrest. He wants Hendee.

And it's then that my gut urges me to sign.

Maybe I feel this way because, right then, my thoughts have stopped on the conclusion that the only reason Hendee could want to leave the country is that his penchant for violence has grown stronger than his instinct to write candid poems. Or maybe it's because Jonas keeps right on looking at me like that.

"You have a pen?" I ask Harnischfeger.

Harnischfeger's face lightens up somewhat. He'll consider me, I guess. He'll consider what I might be able to do for the Bureau in the future, I hope.

He removes from his shirt pocket a retractable fine-point, and I sign with the good blue ink.

"Date it please?" he asks, and I do that.

7

Three hours later, Ethan Hendee is behind bars. Every cable channel on the screen in my temporary digs has it as breaking in extra-large font: SUCCESS KILLER ARRESTED. I'm motionless except for my thumb on the remote, which clicks one channel to the next. Looping through my mind is the thought that had I not signed the affidavit, Hendee might instead be en route to Mexico. I remove "Hope" from my pocket, unfold it, read it in search of a hint of sociopathy.

I find nothing of the sort.

I find myself rereading the three lines that go straight to my heart:

nighttime was out there

Mexico was out there

no one would see shit until sunrise

My FBI smartphone rings. Jonas, I think, and I swipe it open without a glance and say, "Bro."

"Hey!" a bright voice says—maybe Em's.

"Hey," I say with less vivacity than I'd like.

"You don't know who this is, do you?"

"Of course I do."

"You're with another woman—I can sense it!"

The cajoling confirms that it's her. "Hope" is still in my hand.

"Seriously," I say. "It's just me and cable news, sister."

"Then I guess you've heard they arrested your client."

"The reports are calling him that?"

"No, but I heard you talking to him at the Cornelia—remember?"

"You recognized him from then?"

"I recognized him because he was Ethan Hendee."

"Oh," I manage, thrown because she's just underscored what a failure I've been in getting Hendee published. "I didn't know you were that into poetry," I say.

"There's plenty about me you don't know, buster."

In no mood to flirt, I am nonetheless charmed. How does she do this to me?

"Anyway," she says. "I guess I'm calling to let you know I'm flying solo presently also."

"At your place?"

"Actually I'm right down Duane from you. Having a Cobb salad at that really old diner."

"The one with the high tin ceiling?"

"Uh-huh. I love this place. You should join me. Maybe I could cheer you up."

"I kind of doubt that. I mean, I doubt anyone could."

"Because you don't think Ethan Hendee's guilty?"

"I don't know what to think."

"You need company, mister. And for those purposes I'm really not all that bad, am I?"

I feel a smile coming on. "You are not."

"So you'll be here?"

"Sure."

"Then I'll pace myself."

"On what?"

"The Cobb salad!"

She clicks off, leaving me alone with a newscaster who's mentioning my name.

I've "just been released" is the report millions of people are hearing.

Is it coincidence, the newscaster wonders, that Hendee and I have both taken lives rather gruesomely?

I turn off the TV, brush my teeth, splash my face with cold water, pat down my hair, the whiteness of which still shocks me.

Then I leave the apartment and head west on Duane, toward what I realize I will now always think of as "that really old diner."

En route, I open the email app on my FBI phone. The gmail password I used before my twenty-eight minutes, Matt222, still works. Since my release I've received only three queries. Two are from women who present more typos than publishing credits, one from a guy whose pitch line is, "I, too, did time for manslaughter, in my case for killing my mother."

Before those are pages of emails that prove to be, in effect, advertisements for self-publishing.

Your career's over, I think. Get used to it.

I put on my best brave face, walk on. Open the tall glass door to the diner, step inside. Em is sitting in a booth well toward the back. She looks up, gives me a wave, her smile widening her eyes.

What does she see in you? I wonder as I head over. There's no food in front of her, not even a glass of water.

"Where's the Cobb salad?" I ask.

"What Cobb salad?"

"The one you mentioned on the phone."

"Oh." Her expression darkens a bit. She appears well-rested and sober. "That was just…for comic effect to get you down here."

I picture Considine sleeping with Lauren and think, *Lie.*

But almost as soon, Em's shiny black eyes, bright again, have me thinking, *But only a white lie.*

"Well, I'm here," I say.

"Well, I'm pleased to see that."

I slide into the other side of the booth. On the table in front of her are a quarter-inch-high stack of paper, a pencil, and a laptop opened and aimed at her. Dammit, I think. She writes. She likes me because she thinks I can sell her memoir—when she realizes I can't, she'll be gone.

She raises a menu in front of her face, asks, "What are we having?"

"You decide. I'm still struggling with thoughts about Hendee."

"I'm thinking French toast. How do you feel about French toast?"

This question—from her—is undoing the gloom in me.

"With bacon?" I ask.

"Of course!"

She places down the menu. A young waiter appears.

"The French toast," she tells him. "With extra powdered sugar and two sides of bacon. Your thickest slices."

"Will do," he says, and he's gone.

We sit saying nothing. Even in this diner's harsh light, she glows. She's in a tattered Stones T-shirt, still no jewelry, still none needed.

But the laptop. Its presence keeps nagging me with the notion that she wants representation by me. So before I fall any further for her, I need to clear the air.

"What's with the laptop?" I ask.

"This thing?"

"Yes."

"My son wants to Skype. I told him I was busy right now, but the kid insists that we Skype."

"He lives far from here?"

"In Santa Monica."

"Did you want me to leave while you talk?"

"Not at all."

"Do you want me to meet him?"

"Nah," she says, which hurts a little. "He's too busy for us old peeps."

"What's he do?"

"Tech stuff. And he's getting married in six months. Playing the love game young, just like his mum did."

"How young in his case?"

"Twenty."

"Poor fellow. He's in for some ups and downs."

"Yes, he is."

"Here I thought you had the laptop open to do writerly things."

"No. Though I have been reading Jill Klugman's *Paris Review* story." She flips over the stack of paper, and I see that it's a photocopy of a story, the title "Fiercely" centered in bold type.

"Who's Jill Klugman?" I ask.

"That woman we heard reading last night. The talented one."

"Oh. Right."

"You forgot? You're that thrown off by Ethan Hendee being the killer?"

I feel my face lose color: it's only now hitting me, all of me through and through, that my judgment of Hendee was entirely wrong.

"Wait," Em says, "did you not want to talk about him?"

"I don't know. I don't know. I guess maybe I'm *supposed* to talk about him to feel better about all this, but, no, I'd rather not. Not now."

"Can I ask super quickly if you think he did it?"

My FBI phone is turned off, and I'm glad about that. I'd never want the Bureau to know I'd second-guess it.

"Of course, this is all off the record," I say. "But there's still something in me that says he's innocent."

"Really?"

I nod.

"God," she says. "That's horrible."

"Yeah, but what do I know? I've been away for more than four years."

"Did you hear they're saying no way will he be let out on bail?"

I shake my head no. "Because he's a flight risk?"

"That and because it's multiple murders."

I'm unable to move. It's still sinking in.

"Think they'll have you testify at his trial?" she asks.

The waiter returns, sets down two glasses of water, walks off.

"That's what I keep wondering," I say just before I sip.

"If they do, what would you say?"

"That's the question."

"Well?"

"To begin with, I'd say he's the most talented writer I know."

Angelic as Em's face is, it offers an ugly flash of envy.

"You think his stuff's better than this?" she asks, sliding "Fiercely" toward me.

"I do."

"But you haven't read a word of it."

"We heard her read the first half. Which, yeah, I'll admit was good. But not Hendee good."

"Okay, but it gets better at the end. Way better. I think this Jill Klugman is going to end up being huge. And, hey, maybe you could represent her. Why couldn't you represent her? At least read from where the narrator and her guy go over to her uncle's house. I need to set up this Skype so I can at least touch base with my son briefly—so feel free to read while I do what I gotta do?"

"I'll give it a look," I say, and she nods cheerfully at me, if not even a little seductively.

So I take hold of "Fiercely," flip to the second half of it, spot the words "Uncle Gino's," and read:

> But then, on the drive over to Uncle Gino's, I kept ob-sessing on Artie's having sold that bag of heroin to Danny Knolton. I wanted to tell Vince about that but didn't be-cause, as I saw things, it was bad enough that Jack was in the downward spiral he was.
>
> At Uncle Gino's house, my aunt Angie opened the front door. She hugged me for a long time, and I tried to appre-ciate the quasi-motherhood this gesture seemed to offer, and she kissed Vince in a way that suggested she was under the misimpression that he and I were engaged. There were introductions, though Artie and Uncle Gino seemed bolted to their chairs at the kitchen table, much as Artie did offer a wave. And Jack was there, standing directly beside Artie as

if more of a sibling of Artie's than he was of mine. Jack's eyes looked more like slits than ever.

And we, Vince and I, simply kept standing. No one told us to make ourselves at home, so we stayed right there, on the border between the living room and the foyer. For a long minute, only a few glances over landed on us. Everyone else, it seemed, was getting back to what they'd been doing before we'd arrived, which didn't strike me as much. A TV was on. You could hear a broadcaster's voice, a crowd cheering but not raucously. Football—halfhearted preseason football.

"Tell him not to bring out his cellphone," Uncle Gino shouted over at me. He was beyond both the living room and the doorway to the kitchen, pointing at Vince as if angry at him—but kiddingly, I thought. "We don't use cellphones in my house," he called more softly and kindly, now speaking directly to Vince, but his tone was deeper, which led me to believe he was serious. "Make sure he doesn't bring his out," he told me again, and he glared at me, then smiled. Then he shouted, as if to the whole family, "This is all I ask."

And not long after that, I remember, my dad was talking about candy. At first what he was getting at seemed wacky, a byproduct of synapses in a former NFL running back clearly well into dementia, but on the other hand no one else was making conversation, and my mom was gone, this woman who had, for decades, tended to him so loyally. Who'd loved him fiercely, now that I thought about it. What my dad's point was—and he did have a point then, which he did eventually make—was that the taste of candy was something he craved in situations as difficult as this. He was being diplomatic about my mom, actually. He was giving his go-ahead to me, and to anyone else who cared, to broach the subject of her and her death.

But no one was answering him, so he talked on. About which kinds of candy worked "wonderfully" for him when times were tough—about which kinds he liked most. I remember him using the term "hard candies." I remember him saying the phrase "that light green sour apple kind."

Then, as I recall, Artie began leading Jack toward the basement door. That will always be my most vivid memory of that night: Artie opening the door to Uncle Gino's basement stairs and nodding at Jack to lead Jack down. And Vince, who was seated across the living room from me—he'd gone ahead and made himself comfortable on the couch—he was letting his eyes shoot over and stay on mine as he nodded sideways at the basement doorway. His nod was clearly saying, *Confront Jack now?*

And the thing is, I knew he was right. It was up to me to be the one. Who else was going to? I'd always thought my mom would confront Jack someday and thereby make him an All-American guy all over again, but now, of course, that was impossible. And my dad was now clueless when it came to Jack's drug use, and Aunt Angie would never dare acknowledge that anyone related to her had anything to do with drugs. And Artie and Uncle Gino were using Jack to distribute the stuff, so they weren't inclined to confront him about being hooked—so it was up to me.

"Excuse me," I said to Aunt Angie, who'd been telling me about a new farmer's market twenty miles north. "But I kind of need to powder up."

She nodded as I heard Vince call, "Can I talk to you, Marie?"

I glanced over at him, eased toward where he stood, near the open doorway to the basement, which was just off the kitchen.

"Just be honest with the guy," was the only thing he said, and he said it only after he'd closed the door behind us and we'd begun down the basement stairs.

Then we were down there. You needed to pass a washer and dryer to get to Uncle Gino's homemade bar, in front of which Jack and Artie stood. Already you could smell smoke, from heroin, I guessed, because, much as I was no druggie, what I inhaled did not smell like pot—it smelled vinegary. And it wasn't a joint in the hand Jack now held up near his face. It was a pipe, and he was taking a hit from it.

"Jack, what're you doing?" I said. But only Artie looked over. Artie seemed ready to say something sarcastic, but his eyes shifted toward Vince, and because of Vince he said nothing.

Finally Jack's gaze drifted my way, tried to zero in on me. "Coping," he said.

"But...heroin?" I asked.

Jack didn't offer an answer, not even a shrug.

Then, as if my presence had registered in his mind only now, he said, "Want some?"

"Sure, she does," Vince said, and he took the pipe from Jack. Vince was also then using the lighter Artie had handed him, and I thought, What the F's going on?

"Cool," Jack said.

I was out of it now. I was out of this group of three drug-doing men. It was as if Jack and Artie wouldn't care if I disappeared, and now, apparently, Vince wouldn't care either. And I would've kept panicking about this had Vince not taken my hand. Artie was holding the pipe now; Artie was taking a hit, and Vince's hand was squeezing mine, assuring me, I thought, that he'd played along with Jack only to see if what they were smoking was indeed heroin.

Then Vince's hand squeezed mine harder still, as if to say, *Say it. Say what you need to say now.*

So I gathered my wits and said, "Jack, you told me you'd never do that stuff again."

"I did?"

"Yes."

"When?"

"The summer after you stopped playing football."

"I did?"

"Yes."

"Well, that was a long time ago."

"Exactly my point, Jack."

And you could tell from Jack's eyes, from the sprouting in them of a disinterest in me, that my logic had been lost on him. That all he felt was impatience about when he'd next have the pipe. His hand, scabbed on two of its knuckles, reached toward Artie, his eyes wider only to beg Artie to hurry.

"Jack, I'm talking to you," I said.

Artie lit what was left and gave the pipe to Jack, who toked, effortlessly, repeatedly, then offered the pipe my way. I furrowed my brow emphatically to let Jack know I was livid, and Vince held up a finger as if to say, *Hang on* as he pointed at his phone, which he now had out. Vince glanced at me as if to add, *I just have to take this one call*, then walked off toward the northeast corner of the basement. And to be honest, I didn't care what Vince was doing then; sure, I felt slightly abandoned by him, but, right then, mostly all I cared about was Jack. I was beyond upset with Jack; I wanted to scream at Jack about how fiercely I'd once loved him, almost as fiercely, I thought then, as my parents had loved each other, but how he had then gone and ruined all of that by loving heroin more than he loved them and me, but of course my dad and Uncle Gino and Aunt Angie were directly above us upstairs, so there would be no screaming about anything.

"Jack, you are so stupid," was what I did manage to say, and almost as soon, I regretted this. Now I wanted Vince beside me. "I mean," I said to Jack, "you have no idea how stupid you are to be doing this right now."

After all, Jack was almost forty, yet he was acting like he was sixteen. And when I'd been sixteen he'd been so adult—so much wiser than me, so disciplined when it came to what it took to win at the football games he played in, so respectful of my parents and the rules of their house—such an athlete despite the fact that football was already dinging him up, so skilled, so in charge, so seemingly closer to material success compared to me. I wanted to tell him all of this, but his empty expression warned me that none of it would matter; all that mattered to him was that his lungs were now growing full of the relief the pipe offered.

"Just let him," Artie was saying. "For Christ's sake, Marie, his mom just died."

"So did mine, Artie."

Artie shrugged. Smoked.

Screw you, was how I took this.

"Had you guys not been doing this crap back when I was a senior in high school," I said, "you wouldn't have put me—or yourselves—through that night when you and I, Artie, were visiting Jack at UNH."

"Which night?" Artie asked. Jack was watching Artie's mouth, as if both fascinated and relieved by how Artie had pronounced those two words.

"You know which night," I said.

"No, I don't," Artie said snidely.

"The Danny Knolton night," I said, hoping Vince was distracted from hearing us by his phone conversation in that dark northeast corner, but if Vince wasn't—well, so be it.

"Marie, you don't want to know a thing more about that night," Artie said. "Believe me, you don't."

My hands were on my hips, squeezing them. My lips were pursed and I forced them to part to say, "I saw you sell him the shit that killed him, Artie. I saw the baggie. I saw you do it. I was there, remember?"

"I'm telling you, Marie," Artie said. "There's plenty more about that night you don't want to know."

And Jack was eyeing me directly now, as if to ask, *Marie, why are you bringing this up?*

Then Vince—a glance in want of him told me—was on his way back, apparently done with his call. Then he was beside me, then slightly in front of me and between me and Artie and Jack, his phone still in his hand, its screen lit. If he meant to protect me physically from Artie, he was also now facing me and putting himself at risk regarding any punch Artie might try to throw at him from behind. I thought of him—Vince—as being brave then. But then he said, to me but also to Artie and Jack, "Maybe I'd best be going?"

"Why?" I asked.

"I mean, if you'd like me to stay down here, I will," he said to me. "But if you'd rather I leave so you can sort out the rest of these...matters, I'll go upstairs. Your dad said something about candy, so I'm thinking maybe I'll go out and get him a bag. Some of those hard sour apple ones he was talking about? As a gesture of, you know, kindness?"

"Sure," was all I could think to say, because I was flustered; the selfishness of all three of these men had me unglued. I was stone-faced no doubt, hoping Vince would decide that, after all, what he wanted most was to stay as close to me as possible.

But then he was off, headed toward the washer and dryer. I wished he weren't leaving but noticed Artie handing the pipe back to Jack, who, again, was trying to light it.

"Weren't supposed to use your phone anyway," Artie called out to Vince just before Vince hung the right toward the stairs.

Vince stopped briefly then but didn't turn around. He raised his phone over his shoulder, to acknowledge he'd heard. As he continued on, he made a show of sliding the phone into his back pocket, as if telling Artie he believed this should satisfy Uncle Gino's rule, and Artie did seem satisfied, for the time being.

Then there was only the sound of Vince ascending the stairs.

"Decent enough guy," Artie said. But the longer no one spoke, the more it sounded as if he'd been trying to convince himself of this. Then, to me, Artie said, "Would you say?"

"Would I say what?"

"That Vince is a decent guy."

And before I could answer, Jack, flummoxed, was facing the basement's northeast corner, where Vince had been making the call.

Then Artie was facing that corner also. And running over there, shouting, "What the shit—what the shit—Marie, what the shit was this guy of yours doing over here? Jack, do you see this? Jack, look at this—look at what that jackass did! One of the cartons from *Canada* is open! He was snooping, Jack! Marie, who does this guy think he is? He wasn't supposed to even take any calls; you heard my dad—he wasn't even supposed to have his phone out! I let him slide on that for like five seconds, and he comes up with the nerve to do this?"

Jack began past me, to head for the boxes, and I grabbed his arm, the one that wasn't holding the pipe, to try to stop him. My fingernails dug into the skin on that arm, and with my other hand, I grabbed the pipe and felt it burn my palm, but I kept on yanking.

"Give it, Jack!"

"Marie—"

"Give it to me!"

"Jack, do you see this?" Artie was calling. He wasn't quite yelling, probably because he didn't want Uncle Gino to hear, but he was incensed—you could hear the rage in his tone.

And Jack said, "See what?"

Then came the first thing I saw of any of them, a flash from one of their cameras.

Then, almost all at once, dozens more flashes, and before my eyes could adjust to the brightness completely, at least ten of them had streamed well into the basement, all protected by handguns and long guns and bulletproof vests. Most of them wore caps, "FBI" in white over navy blue. Three already had Artie down, face-first against the floor.

Another four were wrestling Jack. My hand was clutching the pipe, trying to hide it, but two of the guys wearing caps were now flanking me, the one to my left saying I was under arrest for possession and had rights, the other grabbing my hand and prying it open while most of the others stood in that northeast corner, shining flashlights into a box.

"Paydirt," one of those others called.

"Booyah," another said.

I pictured Vince, the man I'd now always remember as the agent who'd used me to set up my family, grinning in some FBI van parked less than a mile off. I imagined that, as he'd left the house minutes ago, he'd charmed my dad, too, maybe by saying he was off to buy candy. I wondered if, without my mom around to keep my dad's mind on her and things like family togetherness, my dad was still craving some of that sour green apple taste.

If he is, I thought, can you blame him?

I set down the story, gaze out the tall window beside our table. The coincidence of me and this character Vince both working undercover has me sure Em's onto the fact that I've been working for the Bureau. She showed me "Fiercely" to get me to talk, I imagine. She's already pieced together my early release and Hendee's bang-bang arrest—she's even brighter than I thought.

But if I tell her I've been undercover and the Bureau finds out—which it would—I'll never work undercover again. And, true, Harnischfeger's done using me to get Hendee, but there's always the future. After all, there are plenty of celebs who want book deals, and more of them are up to no good than their adoring fans think.

I continue to say nothing to Em. I watch the passersby on the other side of the tall window as if pensively, pretending to let "Fiercely" register in my heart.

"Well?" I hear. "What do you think?"

The passersby are reading their phones, one after the next. It's sunny out. Then it isn't.

"About what?" I ask.

"About the story, silly."

"To be honest, I was wondering why you wanted me to read it."

"I didn't, necessarily. I just happened to have it here, remember?"

I note how quickly she's gone from sounding openhearted to striking me as actually on edge.

"I guess you did," I say.

"We don't have to talk about it, Matt. I mean, I understand why you wouldn't want to talk about it."

"Why wouldn't I want to talk about it?"

My FBI phone rings. I remove it from my inside pocket, answer it.

"Buddy," Jonas says. "Just wanted to congratulate you personally."

"I'm busy, man."

"With what? Literary stuff?"

"Not really."

"Ah. With Em."

I say nothing.

"Then we'll catch up later," he says. "But just wanted to let you know that Harnischfeger said you can stay in the apartment and use both phones until the end of the month. His way of thanking you."

"In other words, my severance package," I say.

"Well, yeah. If you want to look at it that way. I mean, you did know we needed you to get Hendee, right?"

"Yes. But—"

"Anyway it's not like you and I can't hang out. I mean, it's not like I'm on cases twenty-four seven."

"Right."

"So, yeah, let's catch up later? But for now, bro, gracias. And

I mean that sincerely. For an amateur, you did some damned stellar work."

"Thanks," is all I say, because Em is facing me, apparently curious about who I'm talking to.

"Severance package?" she asks after I hang up.

"That was a joke," I say. "Just me speaking...you know, metaphorically. It's no big deal. It's nothing."

She studies her manicured fingernails, as if considering this.

"Does that mean you're ready to spend a little quality time with me?"

"Isn't that what we're doing?"

Her black eyes rise until they meet mine. "No."

"Ah," I say.

"Ah as in yes, you're up for walking me to your cute little apartment down the block?"

"Yes. Ah as in that."

"And then, once we get inside that cute little apartment, us probably not saying all that much to each other?"

She does not smile, and I like that.

"So we're outta here?" she asks.

"If you are," I say, "so am I."

8

For the record, not long after we leave the really old diner, Em and I prove that, for us, at least for today, physical proximity to each other is aphrodisiac enough.

Also for the record, Ethan Hendee does not have such luck. He's arraigned the following day. He pleads not guilty, but as per a legal expert on cable news, "You always plead not guilty in high-profile capital murder—that's just standard."

In any event, when it comes to Hendee, the Matt Connell I was before my twenty-eight minutes—the successful, respected, sought-after literary agent—has become a ghost. I am a killer and a client of mine is a killer, so there will be no book deals for any writer represented by me.

And Em does not contact me that following day, or the day after that, so I'm receiving essentially no calls, texts, or emails— it's just me and the sawhorses and several men wearing hardhats on that roof I can see out the window.

Then, three days after Hendee's arraignment, I receive a text: *Yo.*

My first thought is it's Em being playful.

But the text isn't from her—it's from Jonas.

And not from his FBI number, so, to speak to him as a pal his age might, I go with the vernacular of some of the convicts I knew who were his age: *Sup.*

And he responds immediately with *Tomorrow's 5:30a ferry to Staten Island. I'll be on it you should too.*

They need me again, I think. They need me!

But of course there's the question of why he's using his own phone.

Still, I text back quickly with *Will be there.*

I barely sleep that night. Em hasn't phoned or texted for almost four days now. Then, thanks to a dearth of cabs anywhere near Duane, I almost miss the 5:30 a.m. to Staten Island.

But I do make it. The last on, but I'm on. As the ferry chugs away from Whitehall Terminal, I hear, "Buddy."

I turn. Jonas is standing alone beneath the stowed flotation devices. He grins. He's wearing jeans and a faded black T-shirt. He seems even younger than he did when I first met him in the yard—this tall, horse-faced, unshaven man here, on this early morning ferry, is doubtless the non-Bureau Jonas.

He points to the starboard side, heads there. I follow him past New Yorkers who couldn't appear more bored. We stand at the rail and face the water.

"What's the story?" he asks.

"You're the full-timer. You tell me."

"Right."

He's apparently reading the sky for the best way to address what's only now dawning on him, the fact that I want to discuss my working for the Bureau for good.

Then he says, "I want to thank you again for all you did to put Hendee away, man. It's easier to screw up undercover than people think, but you...you delivered."

I study the chop on the harbor. It's small but quick and un-relenting.

"Well, you're welcome again," I say, and I notice he's unfold-ing a piece of white paper. This one doesn't look like a xerox of a Hendee poem, and for that I'm grateful. But then I see a laser-printed name, address, phone number all single-spaced in the upper left corner, which, to the literary agent in me, means *manuscript*.

Worse, beneath a title I don't read are single-spaced lines, which mean *poetry*.

And to top it off, the name in the upper left-hand corner is Jonas's.

No, I think. Please no.

"Jonas, what is this?" I ask.

"A little bit of my work. I hope you don't mind?"

"Wait—are you—wait, what're you saying?"

"I was hoping you could read it."

"Are you telling me you brought me out here to read a god-damned *poem* you wrote?"

"I am."

"And you want me to—what did you want me to do?"

"Just read it, bro. Just read it and tell me if you think it's any good. I mean, that's what you do for a living, right?"

"No!"

"No?"

"Not today! No! Not ever again, if I can help it! Jonas, *man*, use your head. A client of mine—and a poet at that—was just arrested for multiple murders! Not to mention, don't you realize that, now that I've had more than four years in a cage to ponder my life, I am so *done* with reading manuscript after manuscript that, on page one, uses the phrase 'the color of a bruise'? And uses it *proudly*? And now here you are—Paul Jonas, who, when I woke up this morning, was the coolest guy I'd ever met—and it turns out you lured me onto this goddamned ferry to show me this fucking…*cinquain?*"

Everyone nearby is backing off. To Jonas's credit, he remains composed. He is now, like me, studying the chop, which is stronger.

He all but whispers, "Two things."

"What?"

"One, it's mostly because of me that you were released from Sing Sing."

He's got a point, I think. *If* he's telling the truth.

"What's two?" I ask.

"Two has been obvious, I thought, from the very god-damned start."

"What is it?"

"Two, Matt, is I would never. *Ever.* Put something as work-shoppy as 'the color of a bruise' in anything I'd write. Poetry or otherwise."

He nods at me, definitely and mightily. Folds his poem,

pockets it. Negotiates his way past people to the other side of the ferry.

And we stay apart like that the rest of the way to Staten Island.

As well as all the way back.

9

Em has quite a place. Two bedrooms and 2,000-plus square feet on the thirty-ninth floor, a southern exposure overlooking Nolito, the Wall Street skyline, and the sparkle on the New York harbor. She's either accomplished something major or been born into some serious family wealth—much as I'm curious about which, it's too early to ask.

I step out of her gargantuan shower, begin drying myself with one of the six designer towels stacked in the designer basket beside her designer sink.

"Matt?" I hear from the living room.

I peer out the bathroom door, patting my chest. "Yes?"

She doesn't look up. Still undressed and wrapped in the comforter she took with her from the bedroom, she sits cross-legged among her designer pillows on her designer living room couch, eyes on a laptop propped up by the insides of her thighs, brow furrowed.

"They found another piece," she says.

"I'm sorry?"

"Of a woman. A fourth victim, apparently."

"You're kidding."

"Nope. And this one's husband says she went missing only three days ago."

"You mean…you're saying she was killed after Hendee was locked up?"

"Yes."

"So he's innocent!" I say, buoyed by glee—only to feel so lightheaded I need to sit.

"That's right," she says. She stays focused on the laptop, as if she knows I signed the affidavit. I want to explain to her that I was confused. Want her to know I saw two padlocked rooms and smelled something odd, and that Hendee was set to flee the country.

But to come clean about this would mean admitting I was undercover—and if she knows I was undercover, I'm worth zip to the Bureau from now on.

"That's some pretty major egg on law enforcement's face," I say.

"You mean on the FBI's face," she says, finally looking over.

"Whoever," I say. "In any case, someone really screwed up."

I get dressed and head toward her nightstand for my FBI phone. It's still angled just as I left it: no reason to believe she's tried to snoop. I open it, check for word from Jonas—texts, dropped calls, whatever. I even log into the Instagram account someone at the Bureau set up for me.

"What're you doing?" she asks.

"Checking in with society."

"I thought you were done with society."

"Not when a client suddenly has ten times the fame he had a week ago."

"I'd say twenty. Easily. He's trending higher than he was when they arrested him—he's number two on Twitter." She's still reading her screen. "And now a headline's saying he's about to be released."

And there goes the ringer for emails on my phone: *ping*.

I open my email account to see a sea of new queries.

I'm an agent again—but unfortunately, a literary one.

I find the button that's supposed to mute the phone, tap it repeatedly until it works. To my chagrin I see that there's nothing from Jonas. Much as I'm probably about to make a nice chunk off a book deal for Hendee, I still want to be a lifer for the Bureau. The Success Killer is out there, and I hate that, and I want foremost to deal with that. Maybe because I've killed and still feel the need to repay my debt. Maybe because I want to put the most hateful writer behind bars—I don't know.

Whatever the reason, I read the memo lines of thirty or so of the new emails. All are queries from writers I've never heard of, except one from Mitchell Parker, who I again believe Jonas should put on the list. I skim Mitchell's query, which pitches his idea for a diet-and-exercise book for middle-aged men. I think, Shit, maybe he *is* innocent.

Then I watch my inbox grow more inundated still.

Come on, Jonas, I think.

But every email that appears is about literary business.

One's from an acquiring editor at a Big Five house, so I open it:

"...we've finally gotten around to finishing our review of the manuscript of Ethan Hendee's poems you submitted several years ago, and we're now in the financial position to be able to offer you the kind of advance Mr. Hendee deserves..."

I open the attached contract, see the figure of $10,000, think: *Ha.*

That's chump change now, my friend, I want to email back.

But the wise move, of course, is to delete the email—to remove all temptation to give in to the offer.

"What ya got there?" Em calls from the island in her kitchen, where she keeps her dispenser of cucumber water.

"Agenty stuff."

"From him?"

"You mean Hendee?"

"Uh-huh."

"No, but I'm sure I'll be hearing from him."

But the truth is that I'm not sure. Isn't it possible Hendee suspects I had something to do with his arrest? Knows it, maybe? Maybe his lawyer told him? Either way, how will he react to all the attention and adoration he's about to get? Will he stay loyal to me, the agent who never landed him a deal? Or go the Blaine Davis route by dumping me for snazzier representation as soon as a nice offer comes his way? He and I haven't even discussed having a contract between us for years—it's all been a gentlemen's agreement, and now, as I feel more uncertain about the path of my future than I did yesterday, that might be coming back to haunt me.

In any case I want to help the Bureau catch the Success Killer more than I want to make books. After all, I was rewriting manuscripts and cutting deals when Lauren cheated on me, and I was with the Bureau when Em decided to give me a try. Maybe I exude something pure when I'm trying to fight crime. Regardless, I could get a call from Jonas at any moment, and if I do, I'll need to talk with him outside of Em's earshot.

"Think I'll take a little walk," I call to her without looking up.

"Need some company?" she asks, and I glance over, her bright black eyes yet again drilling pleasantly into my soul.

"Yes and no," I say. "But maybe a little more of a no for now?"

"Oh," she says, looking off.

And she's making no attempt to hide her disappointment.

I thought she was too cool for disappointment, and now we both know I was wrong.

"Back in an hour at most," I say.

I wait for a sarcastic retort, but all she says is, "Okay."

I nod, though I'm not looking at her. I'm looking at my phone as intently as someone a generation younger than me, hoping to see an email or a text from Jonas.

"But of course," Em adds with sufficient zing, "I can't guarantee you I'll be here."

10

I decide to walk all the way to the apartment on Duane. Or, to continue to be technical, the FBI's apartment on Duane. My phone is still pinging now and then, but most everything is either from an acquiring ed "just checking in" or a query about a manuscript I consider slush upon sight. A good portion of the queries open with words to the effect of *Like you and Ethan Hendee, I've spent time behind bars.*

There's still nothing coming in from Jonas. Or from Harnischfeger. Or from anyone else at the Bureau. Four blocks away from the apartment, I buy a bagel from a bodega and eat it. I realize I'm too jazzed about Hendee's release to enjoy food. I'm inside the building and almost to the apartment door when a call labelled JONAS hits my screen.

This time he's using his FBI number, so all I say to answer is, "Jonas."

He says nothing as I unlock my door and walk in. Then there, inside the apartment, I see him, Jonas, in the flesh, on the no-nonsense couch, his eyes locking in on mine. He lowers his phone, clicks it off.

Asks, "Did you hear?"

"Of course."

"You want back in?"

"Naturally."

"Then we're off to see Harnischfeger. He's talking a new plan since…well, since the old plan obviously didn't work."

"Where does he want to meet?"

"Library again."

"Let's go."

He nods and clears his throat and we're off. We're without conversation in our descent to the lobby. On the sidewalk, hailing a cab, he says, "Can I ask you something?"

"Sure."

"Could you please not mention my poetry?"

"What do you mean?"

"I'm asking you not to tell the Harn that I wrote that cinquain."

"Okay, but why not?"

"Because I'd never hear the end of it."

"You mean from him, or from everyone at the Bureau?"

"From everyone in the world."

A cab squeals to a halt within six inches of us. Jonas, stoic, opens the door to the back seat.

"Remember who we are," he mutters as we slip inside. Meaning we are again supposedly agent and client. Meaning he's again Pat Lynch from Barstow who wrote a novel I adore, and I'm the agent who represents it.

Meaning I'm back with the Bureau and maybe even for good? For two blocks I ponder this question, as well as whether to keep it to myself, while Jonas studies the cabbie and the dayglo stickers of various cartoon monsters on the dashboard, then watches Manhattan blur past us out the window on his side.

At Forty-First and Fifth, we leave the cab determinedly. Jonas pays and tips with cash. We ascend the white marble stairs; no one leaving the library is paying us so much as a glance.

Our strides grow brisk in the gray hallway leading to the small room. Inside sits Harnischfeger and a young woman whose eyes alternately linger on and flit from mine as if she's trying her best to trust me. She's wearing a white blouse buttoned to the top and pants made of black fabric that appears neither expensive nor cheap. Her posture is somehow better than Harnischfeger's. The confidence she exudes suggests that she, too, has a proven ability to take a human life without weaponry.

"Gentlemen," Harnischfeger says.

Jonas and I nod, each bring a folding chair into what's now a tight circle of four.

"This is Trinko," Harnischfeger says to me.

"Dawn, correct?" I ask, and I step toward her to shake, but she waves me off and points her chin at my chair.

As I sit she says, "Feel free to call me Trinko."

"You two met over the phone, right?" Harnischfeger asks, and she nods his way, and I respect her for being all business, but mostly for landing a full-time gig with the Bureau. She stands, removes a phone similar to mine from her pocket. Silently reads its screen, glances at Harnischfeger, holds up a finger, then leaves the room for the gray hallway, closing the door behind her.

Harnischfeger continues:

"You should know right off the bat, Matt, that what was found in the case of this fourth victim was a hand, but this time it wasn't found floating in the East River. Homeless guy found it digging through a trash bin. Guy comes up with a crumpled McDonald's bag, opens it, undoes the wrapper around what he figures is an intact burger, takes one bite and boom—a writer's hand is in his mouth."

"We're sure it's a writer's hand?" I ask.

Jonas points directly at me and says, "About as sure as we can be. Because there's a tattoo on the back of it, of one italicized word: *Revise.*"

"Meaning it was...that woman who read at the Cornelia?" I ask. "Jane Klugman?"

"*Jill* Klugman," Harnischfeger says.

"So now everyone at that reading is a suspect," Jonas says. "Including your lady friend Em."

Harnischfeger looks over at me, gauging my reaction, my mind rushing into a blur of thoughts about Em's having read and made a copy of Jill's story, about her arguable envy of Jill for having written it, about how, because she showed it to me and asked me what I thought of it, she might be on to the fact that I'm with the Bureau.

"Lucky for us, the guy went to NYPD," he says. "But the

point is, Matt, when it came to this fourth victim, the killer decided to go with making the pieces he's disposing of smaller."

"Why?" I ask. "Fear?"

Harnischfeger nods.

"And can I ask what's probably a very stupid question?"

"By all means," he says. "As you're probably already learning
well, Matt, the Bureau is for shit without the asking of the stu-
pidest of questions."

I nod. "Okay then. Are we sure the killer is a he?"

"Trinko's saying the chances of him being male are now up
to ninety-seven percent."

Good, I think, relieved.

But only ninety-seven percent relieved, because already my
mind's off into a whirl of worry, about how I should probably
mention that Em might have been envious of Jill, about how,
if I do, Em will likely become a suspect, about how that would
end my quality time with her—and about how, dammit, I'm
crazy about her.

"Anyway now we're looking into your client Mitch Parker,"
Harnischfeger says. "Is there anything, let's say, notable about
him you'd like to share?"

"Right off the bat I'll say I never really did like the man."

"Was there a particular reason for that?"

I shrug. "He was just so damned full of himself. Even for a
writer."

"Anything else?"

"He emailed me recently."

"About?"

"A diet-and-exercise book."

"Anything striking about that query? Anything angry, cynical—interpretable as violent? Maybe an uncommon concentra-
tion of typographical errors?"

"Not that jumped out at me. But I can forward the email to
you."

"Do that," Jonas says.

"Forward that to me and Trinko," Harnischfeger tells Jonas.

"Mitch has always been an odd guy period," I say. "I'm not sure which way that cuts."

"He never said anything misogynistic to you?" Harnischfeger asks. "Or anything at all that suggested a deep level of frustration with women?"

"I never knew him to date anyone," I say. "Which I've always figured was because he was so selfish he lacked charm altogether. Does that suggest frustration on his part? It would for me if I were him."

The door to the hallway opens.

Trinko walks in sliding her phone into her pants pocket.

"She had no book contract," she tells Harnischfeger. "The husband says he's sure of that."

"So fine then," he says. "We're no longer looking for the Success Killer. Maybe this monster has a literary bent to him, but I'd say we now refer to him as the Lady Killer."

Jonas, I realize, is studying me again. Harnischfeger has fallen silent, Trinko rechecking her phone.

"What?" I ask Jonas.

"Nothing," he says. "Other than how 'bout you give us your gut feeling on Jill not having a contract? I mean, given what you know about literary folk in the city?"

Come off as smart, I think. If you want to stay on with the Bureau, come off as invaluable.

"My thought," I say, "would be that she might have been killed because, in the perp's eyes, she was one step away from signing a big deal too."

"We don't use the word perp," Trinko says. "That's just what they call them on TV."

"So in your estimation, Matt," Harnischfeger says, "are you suggesting that maybe we use the name the Talent Killer?"

I nod, and he glances over at Trinko, who says, "He makes a decent point."

"The Talent Killer it is then," Harnischfeger says. "And with that in mind, Matt, I'm going to ask you to do something for us that I think your email inbox will help you with."

"What's that?"

"Pursue all manner of contact with every *untalented* novelist in the tristate area. The more untalented, the better."

"In other words," Jonas says, "be a literary agent who's supposedly separating the wheat from the chaff, but your goal is to find the worst chaff."

I nod.

"Here," Trinko says, eyeing her phone. "Here's something. Jill Klugman's sweater was just found one trash bin over on Riverside. And it was missing the top button. And the husband's saying that, last he saw her, she was wearing that sweater, and that that button was *not* missing."

"The husband's a suspect, I take it?" I ask.

"Crying his eyes out while he and I were on the phone," Harnischfeger says. "Dawn's put his percent chance of being our man at probably less than ten. Less than five, in my opinion, given how he's been cooperating with us."

"In any case, gentlemen," Dawn says, "the button was silver, round and, in the husband's words, *domelike*. Which I'm taking to mean no holes in the facade itself, a loop underneath for the thread to go through."

"What color was the thread?" I ask.

"Good question," she says. "Hang on."

And with that she types something, presumably that question, and sends it off.

Then we all four sit.

Jonas, I notice, fidgets a bit now and then.

Finally, Trinko looks up.

"Eggplant," she says.

"That's a kind of purple, bro," Jonas tells me.

"I know that, bro," I reply as kindly as I can.

"The color of the thread notwithstanding, Matt," Harnischfeger says, "your task now is to zero in on the least promising literary talent you can find. I'll add a couple grand to the balance on that debit card, which you'll continue to treat, as you use it around anyone, whether they're a suspect or not, as if it's attached to your own personal account."

I nod.

"Sound fine?" he asks.

I realize that, right now, I could try to negotiate for more cash. But I don't want more cash. I want primarily to work full-time for the Bureau.

"Yes, it does, sir," I say. "Will let you all know if I come across anything at all angry or violent. Should I forward it to... should I forward it to you in specific?"

"Forward it to all of us," Trinko says, and she looks down at her phone and taps its screen. "I'm sending you our email addresses."

So I'm back, I think. I'm *back*.

11

H ow was society?" Em asks. She's still on her couch, still wrapped in her comforter and, presumably, nothing else.

"Fine," I say.

"Legs stretched sufficiently?"

"Aplenty."

"And Hendee—has he gotten in touch with you?"

"No, but a few other bigshots have. In fact, Blaine Davis just emailed."

"As in the bestselling blockbuster Blaine Davis?"

I nod.

"What was he emailing about?"

"He and Lauren want to have dinner."

"*Your* Lauren?"

"No. His. You did know that, right? That he married her when I was in prison?"

Em sits up straighter. Glances at me incredulously, then collects herself to appear as if she's known about Lauren and Blaine all along.

Then, more herself, it seems, she says, "No. I did not know that. But why—how? How did something like that happen?"

"I used to represent him. You knew *that*, right?"

"Wait. You? You represented Blaine Davis?"

I nod.

"When?"

"When he was coming up. I sold his breakout book."

"*Night of the Solstice.*"

"Yes. And this stays between you and me, sister, but ninety percent of that book was written by yours truly."

Em's entire being goes still. The comforter's fallen somewhat loose, but not a bit of her moves, apparently not even to breathe.

"You're shitting me."

"Nope."

"You wrote *Night of the Solstice?*"

I nod.

"I adored that book! It *sung* to me!"

Good, I think. Maybe she'll stick around?

"But hang on," she says. "If you wrote it, why aren't you the rich and famous one?"

"Because that, my dear, is how NYC publishing works."

She scrunches up her face, maybe feigning ignorance, maybe not.

I say, "As soon as I finished writing that book and sold it for big bucks—well, to be clear, I *re*wrote for him, but also to be clear, I essentially rewrote it from scratch—anyway, as soon as he made it big, he dumped me for an agent at ITM."

"ITM the mega agency."

"Correct."

"The one that represents people like Tom Cruise and therefore has all the clout."

I nod.

"So Blaine just...*dumped* you."

"Yes."

"There was no contract?"

"I've tended to be more of a handshake man."

"And then he also goes and marries your wife."

"Ex-wife, but yes."

"That's just horrible, Matt. Not to rub it in, but that's just about as horrible as it gets."

"To be fair to the guy, she'd already slept with my pal Consee. So, really, by the time my trial was over and I was put away upstate, did I really care what she did? I mean, when you stop to think about it, a woman in that situation should probably move on, right?"

Em takes a long look out her largest window. A seagull zips past. She glances back at me darkly, maybe sullenly.

"I suppose," she says.

"But to get back to Blaine's dinner invitation, I'm thinking of saying yes. Because the thing is, if I do land Hendee a decent contract, which of course is assuming *Hendee* doesn't dump me for ITM, I might be back in the game as an agent in this city. But one big book contract ain't gonna be enough for me to retire on."

"So you don't want to steal back Lauren. You want to steal back Blaine."

I shrug. "Not necessarily. *But...*if I can stomach having dinner with him while he's being all lovey-dovey with Lauren, it won't hurt for me to schmooze with the guy, especially if they invite over anyone else. I mean, he does pal around with lots of huge names."

"Like who?"

"The Kardashians, Clooney, the Baldwins. And that's just who he hung out with before I was sent upstate."

Em's eyes widen.

No, I think. Not another one falling for Blaine.

"Want me to come with?" she asks. "To help you stomach seeing him being all lovey-dovey with Lauren?"

I stare her down as if to say, *Don't play me for stupid.*

"What?" she says.

I realize that the answer I give her right now can steer us toward being one of those couples who never quite tells the truth, who instead play cat and mouse games about how they feel.

"Do you want me to be completely honest?" I ask.

"Were you always completely honest with Lauren?"

"We were like most couples—you know, honest with the occasional white lie."

"Which of course pile up over time."

"Yes."

She nods. "That's how I was with my ex. Should you and I

maybe learn from our mistakes and now go with completely honest?"

I remember her white lie about the Cobb salad in the diner on Duane, how it sent my mind into thoughts I could have done without.

I hold her eyes with mine and say, "I'm game."

"So am I. So go ahead. Be completely honest. Tell me what you were thinking."

"Okay. To be completely—and embarrassingly—honest, I was figuring you want to meet Blaine so you could see if you could get him to hit on you."

Her mouth falls open the tiniest bit.

God, is she ever beautiful.

"To be completely honest," she says, "maybe I was. But let me add this: If there's any celeb I want to meet right now, it's Ethen Hendee. Not to mention, the only reason I'd want Blaine *or* Hendee to hit on me would be so I could see if you like me."

"But you know I like you."

"I do?"

"Of course you do."

"Do I know you like me enough to want to show me off to Blaine and Hendee?"

"Show you off? Isn't that something that—I dunno, jerks do?"

"If it is, I'd be showing you off too."

"To Lauren?"

"Of course to Lauren. Who else?"

"So do you?" I ask.

"Do I what?"

"Want me to bring you to their dinner party?"

She nods and grins eagerly. "You know it, Mr. *Night of the Solstice.*"

"Okay then," I say.

"Okay then," she says. "*Okay.* Looks like—looks like we're on."

12

The emails pour in. It's hard to separate a really bad writer from a really bad writer who might have murdered someone. And sometimes there are excellent writers who've created extremely violent storylines and I'm not sure whether to forward their work or not—occasionally I'm tempted to keep their queries to myself and simply represent them.

I'm also prone to eyestrain when I read queries on my bells-and-whistles phone. As the days pass, I increasingly need to stop and blink hard a few times, as well as take a few deep, calming breaths through my nose. Headaches force me to recline, sometimes on the floor. On the bed I shared with Em, I try to avoid thoughts of her. Of how much I've enjoyed simply talking with her. Of how, to end up with her, I need to do my best to play things cool and wait for her to call me before I call her.

Around noon three days after she and I last saw each other, I get a call, from her, I hope, but it's from Hendee, who, I'm guessing, has gone on to sign with another agent. This call, I believe, will prove to be his goodbye.

"Hend," I say. "Don't worry about letting me down easy; I can—"

"These women!" he says. "I can't believe these women!"

"What?"

"Ever since I got sprung! They won't leave me alone!"

Then I'm smiling because he's laughing—at least we're still friends, I figure. I say, "I'm not sure, Hend, but I think this might be a thing."

"Oh, it's a thing," he says.

And this time as he laughs, I laugh along wholeheartedly.

"But precisely what is it," he asks, "about a guy's having been behind bars?"

"You're saying it's working better for your social life than being a poetry god?"

"Ten times better. It's ridiculous, man. It's great, but it's ridiculous."

"You meet anyone you like?"

Hendee goes quiet, and I think, This is it. This is where I learn he's cut me loose.

"Actually, I have," he says. "Her name is Doreen. Is that even a name anymore—*Doreen?*"

"If she says it's her name, Hend, it's her name."

"But I'm worried about her motives. She's a publicist at Shannon and Dunne. I take it you've gotten that offer they made?"

I go tongue-tied. Does he still consider himself my client?

I manage to say, "In fact I've heard nothing from Shannon and Dunne. And as you know, I haven't heard from you either, so I figured you were long gone."

"What do you mean? You haven't received my calls?"

"No. Not a one."

"That's weird," he says. "Because I've tried calling you—I don't know—half a dozen times? I even texted you! I figured that now that you caved about using a smartphone, maybe you're all of a sudden one of those text-only people."

"No, Hend. Still me. And I'm telling you, not a thing here from you, or from Shannon and Dunne. And for the past few days I've been looking at this phone pretty much nonstop."

"Well, you're hearing from me now. And Shannon and Dunne made me an offer. And Doreen and I have been hitting it off. Do you think that's bad?"

"To be hitting it off?"

"With someone who works for the same publisher who's making the offer."

"It's without doubt a conflict of interest, my man. But this *is* publishing, right?"

Hendee laughs more carelessly than I've ever heard him

laugh. It's in him now: thirty years of typing and mailing out poems has finally paid off in happiness.

"Anyway what was their offer?" I ask.

"Two hundred fifty K for two books, the first a collection of poems, the second a novel."

"A novel?"

"They're telling me I'll be a natural. And I'm not sure you knew this, but I'd been playing around with a new novel before my...you know..."

"Arrest?"

He laughs again, volcanically, almost cackles. For a second I worry he's losing his mind. Is it possible he killed the first three women and someone else killed the fourth?

"So what do you think?" he asks. "Should we sign with S & D, or did you get some other offers?"

"I've been putting off invitations for lunches with eds," I say. "Playing hard to get."

"Uh-huh."

"Let me make some calls. Two-fifty isn't bad, but with this Doreen palling around with you as much as she's been, you might not be thinking too clearly."

"Are you saying what I think you're saying?"

"I'm saying seven figures isn't out of the question, my friend."

"You're serious?"

"I am. So let's hold on, Hend. Let's let them feel their hunger for you for maybe a day or so more, then have me call them and do my thing. Sound okay?"

"Sure. And, hey, it occurs to me you and I never signed a contract. And that maybe, considering how Blaine Davis screwed you over by leaving you, it's time that we sign one."

He doesn't know you signed the affidavit, I think, and I feel horrible about that.

"You do realize that there's some stigma attached to me now, right?" I ask.

"Because you were in Sing Sing?"

"Yes."

"Of course I realize that. And for whatever reason, there's apparently always been stigma attached to me too. So let's make it official, man. Two peas in a pod, you and me through thick and thin forever—regardless of what either of us has done in the past. The Two Bad Boys, bad to the bone. I mean, hey world: watch out for us."

13

Blaine Davis owns a swanky four-bedroom penthouse in Long Island City, Queens, where, now, high rises are replacing warehouses and crumbling pre-war apartment buildings, some of the high rises already blocking the views of Manhattan others of them boasted only months ago. Years ago, Blaine invested his proceeds from *Night of the Solstice* in numerous abandoned warehouses and often-empty parking lots in Long Island City on a tip he'd gotten from a guy named Marty, held onto the deeds for longer than most investors would, then sold half to a developer who promptly built a seventy-six-floor, mirror-windowed finger to Manhattan, the largest penthouse suite in which Blaine owns now free and clear—and lives in with none other than the woman known to me as my ex.

This evening, the six chairs at that penthouse's fashionably narrow dining room table are occupied, the three facing lower Manhattan by Em and me and Hendee, who I've just signed as my client in perpetuity. Blaine and Lauren and Doreen sit across from us, backdropped by glare from the setting sun.

Much as Em's natural beauty continues to have a solid hold on me, Lauren still has looks that could kill. She's had work done since my conviction but still strikes me as exquisite, her hair piled high in that seemingly careless way only women with features stunning as hers can pull off, her teal eyes as mesmerizing as they were the night we met.

Doreen's charms are a different matter. To put it mildly, Doreen is well-endowed. (Or as Em put it in a whisper to me just before we sat, "Damn, are those huge.") Unlike Lauren and Em both, Doreen has a quick smile and a generous, infectious laugh. Her diction confirms her MA in Lit from Harvard, yet she appears enamored of Hendee's plainspoken work, if not his prison haircut and newly acquired tendency to grin. Indeed, Hendee appears happier than he has since the day I met him.

For his part, Blaine has been laying it on thick with Em. He plied her with extra champagne just after we arrived, then with his "imfamous"—his word—martinis, and now, as we eat, he's refilling her glass with pinot. The main course is shrimp something or other delivered by a "copter" to the helipad twenty-six feet above us. If his ego was soaring when he left me for ITM, he's twice as full of himself now.

And Em, to my frustration, is doubtless charmed by him. She's also drunk, so I'm giving her a break on the flirtation escalating between her and him, trying to convince myself it's more his doing than hers.

"Ethan," Lauren now says after her own sip of pinot. "We hear you've been made some offers."

Hendee swallows a mouthful of salad. "This is the word."

"Got yourself a pretty sweet deal, huh," Blaine says, assessing Hendee with what strikes me as a half-hearted attempt to appear impressed.

"It's only two books," Hendee says. "And one of them is poetry, so, well, I'm not sure we're talking about two bestsellers here."

"Still," Lauren says. "That's exciting."

But she's not looking at Hendee. She's looking at me. And an unshod toe under the table, hers, is running up my shin, which reminds me of the length of her legs, which she knows turned me on when we were married. On Blaine's sound system, Marvin Gaye is singing "Mercy Mercy Me," and I can't say I'm not feeling the wine.

"You're representing this deal, Matt?" Blaine asks.

"Who, me?" I say, distracted as per above.

"No, Doreen," Blaine says, and everyone laughs.

Then Lauren, with her eyes still on mine, says, "Of course you."

On top of which she takes her time sipping more wine.

"Yes, he is," Hendee says to Blaine. And ever my pal, he adds a fun little dig: "In fact, we're all signed up to stay true to each other for life."

Blaine brushes this off by glancing my way. "How much are they offering him, Matt?"

Lauren's foot edges higher, past my knee. "It's up there," I say to Blaine. "It's in an area that's so high we want to keep it secret."

Doreen beams. Blaine catches Em's eye and winks at her, and she smiles at him, somewhat perfunctorily, but then her eyes hold his as she, too, sips more pinot.

My FBI phone vibrates. I remove it from my pocket, swipe it open: JONAS.

I let the call go to voicemail. Hoping Jonas will soon text instead, I lean back to hold the phone between the tabletop and my lap and watch the screen long enough that I'm sure I'm being noticed if not considered rude. Lauren's foot continues to go to town just above one knee, then the other. It's pleasant, what she's doing, sexy, sure, but mostly I'm enjoying it because it implies that, in her mind, when it comes to Blaine versus me, I'm winning again.

I look up and glance at her and she allows herself to smile the kind of smile that assures me her foot's presence on my lap is by no means an accident. Complicating matters is that she's far more aware of me than is Em, who's now laughing wholeheartedly with Blaine about some pathetic double entendre about fresh cherries.

Then in comes a text from Jonas:

Where the F are you?

I type as quickly as I can: *Dinner.*

Lauren's foot now rests against the inside of my thigh, her toes kneading it while Jonas and I text nonstop:

You're not at the apt on Duane. Does this mean you're with Em?

Yes.

Get away from her asap and I'm serious.

Why?

Will explain next we speak privately hopefully soon.

Will do my best. Am in Queens.

Why the hell Queens?

Right?

Anyway she's no longer your biz.

Meaning what?

Is she there? Can she see your phone right now?

Blaine, I notice, is making eyes at Em, who sips more wine while studying him.

Nope, I type, and I hit send.

Blaine refills Em's glass, and Lauren's toes inch higher up my thigh. Em laughs loudly at something Blaine said, too loudly, I think, and my mind goes off into memories of Lauren's high-pitched denial of having slept with Considine, of me storming over to Considine's place, of me pounding on his door, of the damned near perfect look of innocence on his face just after he opened that door and said, "What's up?"

Stop! I want to shout at everyone, myself included, and to prevent that and save face, I close my eyes and take a deep breath. Jonas, I'm sure, is wrong if he thinks Em's a suspect—though he's right, I tell myself, that I should leave her alone, and then I open my eyes to see words appear on my screen:

Get back to Manh call me asap.

I exhale slowly as I type and send *Will do.*

And when I look up, Em and Blaine are both watching me, guilty looks on their faces. Hendee and Doreen, I notice, are gone. They're out on the balcony, wine glasses in hand, underlit by the sparkle leaping off the East River, grinning at each other like high schoolers. Em and Lauren are leaving their chairs, too, headed off to somewhere behind me, Lauren giving Em directions to the guest bathroom before simply leading her down the hall.

So it's only Blaine and I, and he wastes no time in asking, "Why aren't you answering my emails?"

"From this afternoon?"

"Yeah."

"I guess I just figured I'd see you. As you can imagine, I've been a little busy since Hendee got out."

"Well, I hope you've taken care of business, because now I need you to do me a little favor."

"What's that?"

"Give some feedback on my next book."

"Why me? Why not your editor? Why not, dare I say, your agent?"

Blaine shrugs, and I have a good idea about what this shrug means. It's the shrug of a proud bestselling author whose publisher won't release the second half of his latest advance because the manuscript he's written hasn't met her satisfaction.

"Anyway, you know I can't do that, Blaine."

"Why not?"

"Because I don't represent you."

"Oh, come on, man," he says. "Just do your thing. Just a little more of that fine rewriting we both know you're still so darned proud of. Think of how good it'll feel to know *more* prose you've written is selling millions of copies."

I'm blinking uncontrollably, remembering how quickly I lost my mind after Consee said *What's up?* and I said *You know what's up* and he said *No, I don't think I do,* and I tell myself that, now, what I need most is to stay calm.

"I already know how that kind of success feels," I say.

"So then do it for old times' sake, man. Come on. Do your old buddy a favor."

I hold up a hand and, quietly as I can, say, "Just stop. Just stop talking about this, okay? It ain't gonna happen, man, so just save us both the trouble and stop talking about it."

He sits back in his chair, looks down at his plate, studies it.

"Fine," he says. "As you and I both know, Matt, everyone has a price, so let's simply figure out yours."

"What're you talking about?"

"You know what I'm talking about."

I look out the window. Hendee and Doreen are kissing, and, for reasons I don't understand, I feel profoundly sorry for them.

"You dismiss ITM as your representation in writing, with me cc'd," I say, "and we'll talk about me representing you at thirty per cent."

"That's ridiculous, Matt."

"That's how much you need me to write this next book of yours, as I see it."

Blaine flinches.

Then, as he tries to collect himself, he sits so far back in his chair it tilts precariously. Then he has himself steadied, and he's shaking his head no.

"Matty," he says.

"What."

"You've got yourself a lovely woman there. I'm sure she wouldn't mind if you brought in some good tax-free cash."

"She's got money of her own."

"Then why is she asking me for free publishing advice?"

"She is?"

"You didn't know this?"

"No. And I don't believe you. Why would she ask you? And how? When?"

"Regarding why, maybe she sensed you weren't...*up* to it?"

I roll my eyes theatrically.

"I have a knack for that, you know," he says. "Supplying women of yours with the very thing you're not giving them quite enough of."

"Now you're just being an ass."

"Regarding how, are you telling me you didn't know she's been emailing me? I figured you knew about *that*. I figured she couldn't have gotten ahold of my email address otherwise."

She's been in your phone, I think.

How many texts has she read? I wonder.

Does she know for sure I'm with the Bureau?

Laughter rings out from the balcony, from Doreen and Hendee both.

"You're bullshitting me about Em," I say.

"I'm offering you a quarter of a million in cash," Blaine says.

"To do nothing but rewrite a stinking novel every fan of mine will buy no matter what."

"Not if it doesn't get past that satisfaction clause, brother. Obviously Sherry's finding it so poorly done she's decided she doesn't want a thing to do with you. A million in cash and I'll consider it."

"Four hundred grand."

"A million and a half."

"Three hundred grand. Do you see how this works, Matty? The longer you negotiate, the more you lose. You, my friend, have the worst poker face in the world."

"You think so?"

"I know so."

"Then I guess we'll see about that," I say, and I slip my phone into the front pocket of my blazer, push myself away from the table, and stand.

"What are you gonna do?" Blaine asks. "Lose your temper? All things considered, jailbird, I'm not sure that would be the best idea for you."

"My temper's fine," I say. And then, convinced that I'm in complete control of my volume, I call toward the hallway, maybe a little too loudly, "Em? You about ready to head out?"

14

On Park Avenue, in front of Doreen's building, as soon as Hendee and Doreen are out of the cab and gone, I turn off my phone in hopes that doing so will keep the Bureau from hearing what I'm about to say—that's how much I don't trust myself.

I close my eyes, tell myself to deal with one thought at a time.

Then I face Em directly and, despite myself, these words come out:

"Why are you asking Blaine for freaking publishing advice?"

She stares straight ahead, through the windshield, supposedly at something uptown.

We absorb jarring rattles thanks to roadwork being done.

Finally, softly, she says, "What are you talking about?"

"Blaine told me."

"Told you what?"

"That you've been asking him."

"Asking him for what?"

"Like I just said, for publishing advice."

"Why would I—Matt, that's simply not true."

I sigh.

Stop, I think.

This will only ruin things.

Stop.

But then here I am going on:

"Then why did he say it, Em?"

"I don't know. You're the one who's friends with the guy."

"And why were you looking in my phone?"

"I was *not*—Matt, seriously, how are you coming up with this shit?"

Stop it, I think.

It's not worth it.

Even if you win this, what would be the prize?

But there I go again, asking, "And now, on top of all that, you're *lying* to me?"

"I am *not* lying. If for no other reason than I'm not the lying type. And we said we wouldn't lie, remember?"

"You lied about the Cobb salad."

"That was for goddamned *fun!*"

"And then of course there's your other bullshit."

"What other bullshit?"

"When we were leaving your place this evening—when you were all *honest* in admitting you were still worried about me maybe having it for Lauren, when clearly you didn't give a *shit* about whether I still had it for Lauren because clearly all you cared about was putting your tenterhooks in Blaine."

"*Tenterhooks.* Who in hell but a man who feels insecure uses *that* word? Plus I had no such intentions with Blaine."

"Right. You just happened to be smiling at the guy to no end while sipping his alcoholic beverages seductively."

"I was not sipping seductively. And, hey, Mr. Violent Ex-Con, can't a woman goddamned *smile?*"

I manage to go silent. I need to because it isn't slowing down. Because I need it to stop or change course or who knows? Because I hate having my kind of brain. Hate the fact that if I don't have such a brain, she has me believing I do—and now this belief, in this very argument with her, has me losing to her.

Then I'm keeping my thoughts silent because I'm embarrassed about having started this, about the petty manner in which I did. About Consee having screwed Lauren, about how the fact of that can still sometimes consume me, about how I know that's why I enjoyed feeling Lauren's foot inch its way up my thigh: I am damaged goods, meaning maybe at heart I am no good. I wish I'd never met Lauren, or Consee, or Blaine. I wish I'd never cared about the writing and selling of books. I wish Em would tell me what she wishes and what she wants to forget, maybe needs to forget—but she's still not talking, and, given how dispassionately she continues to sit there, she won't be any time soon.

"And maybe consider the fact that Blaine's the one you're probably angry with, not me," she says.

"I've already considered that. So there's no need to discuss it. So let's not dodge what's going on right now between you and me."

"He's no friend of yours, you know."

"You think I don't know this?"

"I think you've given him the benefit of the doubt far too much. I think he gets off on playing you for a fool. In fact, I sort of know he does."

"Oh, so now I'm a fool? And *he's* the smart one, as are *you*, and I need *you*, this woman who just showed up in my life a few days ago, to tell me how it is—because why? Because she's read the latest issue of the effing *Paris Review*?"

She purses her lips tightly, keeps them that way. She turns to look away from me, straight out the window to her right, her mind maybe running off with thoughts of her own while mine won't stop asking me: *Seriously, where does she get her nerve?*

Seriously, I keep thinking.

Seriously.

Calm down, I think.

This is Ferrari brain.

This is not really you.

This is just what happens to you.

But Ferrari brain was her idea, I think.

And who the hell is she anyway? And why do you trust her? Because you like how she looks and she's got some goddamned wit? Because she's good in bed? If so, admit it: She's not that good. Not Lauren good.

And how stupid are you to trust her after what happened between Lauren and Consee? Huh? Don't you learn from your mistakes? Will you be naïve about women and love and life until you die even though you spent years behind bars supposedly rethinking again and again all the lessons you've learned by fucking up majorly?

And look at Lauren now, going after you again. With Blaine sitting five feet away from her. Does anyone *learn?* No *one learns.* No one. No *matter how cool anyone is at the beginning of the night, at the beginning of the love, at the beginning of their life. Look at Em herself, Ms. Cool, Ms. Above-It-All*—you thought—*flirting with Blaine. Mr. Jackass. Mr.* Night of the Solstice—*how goddamned pretentious of a title is that, anyway?*

And what the fuck's wrong with you for even being in contact with him now that you're out? You don't need him. You only loved Lauren once upon. And once upon is for fairy tales, and fairy tales are always, always fiction.

But the money, you ass.

You need him because of the money.

You're as bad as anyone out there, Blaine and Lauren and Em included—you're acting like a fool because you are weak, and you're weak for the same reason anyone's weak: because you need the money.

My phone vibrates.

JONAS.

Again I let it go to voicemail.

Give a glance over at Em, who's still looking straight out that window to her right.

Though her posture may have lost some of that cold stiffness it had when she went quiet.

If she's been in my phone like Blaine implied, does she suspect that this call was from the Bureau?

If so, is she keeping her mouth shut because she senses the Bureau thinks she's the Success Killer?

I glance over more pointedly, hoping she'll notice.

Say something, I think, but no way will she speak, and now, I promise myself, no way will I.

She's as bright as ever, though. All of her, and I still love that, but that doesn't mean I love her—*that you should know because you're an ex-con who's done more than four in Sing Sing.*

Toughen up, Vitamin-D-Dawg.

Keep your trap shut—toughen your convict ass up.

Again my phone vibrates.

It's gotta be Jonas—why even bother to look?

"Drop me off on Duane, please," I say. "Two-fourteen Duane. Then take this upstanding woman wherever she wants to go, even back to Queens, if she'd like."

The cabbie nods, accelerates, remains as wordless as Em. Why I pressed on with that last twist of sarcasm about Queens bothers me. Fleetingly. Then not at all for at least three blocks. Then intensely for at least six.

And Em's still making a point of looking directly away from me.

Underscoring that whatever's going on in her mind, whether she has Ferrari brain or not—whether there *is* such a thing as Ferrari brain or not—has no foreseeable end.

No end for you, I think.

Not here.

God, does she strike me as dazzling.

God, do I wish she would talk.

15

To my disappointment, Jonas is not on the stoop. Nor is he inside on the stairs I climb to the fourth floor. Nor in the apartment, where I splash water on my face.

I phone him.

"Hey," he says. "You back?"

"Yes."

"At the pad?"

"Yes."

"Stay there. I mean, be outside. I'm on my way."

I hang up and step to the window beyond the foot of the bed. The silver roof out there is eerily moonlit, the workers of course gone for the night. I have no idea what the point of their work is. I leave the apartment and head down.

Outside, a couple walks by, neither holding a phone, though they aren't speaking to each other either. Nor are they holding hands, or in stride. I watch them approach the end of the block and hang the left downtown.

I'm pondering their future when Jonas shows up.

"Brother," he says.

"J-man."

"You look shitfaced."

"I'm fine."

"Then let's take a walk."

"Where to?"

"Tenth Avenue. This far downtown, there's no one there this time of night."

We begin heading west. We haven't gone a block when he asks, "What the hell were you doing in Queens?"

"Having dinner."

"With a shitty writer?"

"With Blaine Davis."

"He's no shitty writer. He's a great writer. You're supposed to be investigating the shitty ones."

"He's very shitty. Trust me."

"I'm serious, Matt. I'm trying very hard to keep you on this case and out of Sing Sing, so don't go getting wacky on me."

"I'm not. I'm telling you: Blaine Davis is a shitty writer."

"Matt, he's an international bestseller. And if you don't stay away from him and the other celebs you know, Harnischfeger will think you're disobeying orders. In fact if I were you, I'd work up a list of at least thirty insanely incompetent writers of violent prose as soon as you get back to the apartment, so you can prove to Harn you've been on top of things. Rather than, you know, living the high life."

I consider mentioning that I wrote *Night of the Solstice*. I'd like to explain how amateurish it was beforehand. I consider theorizing aloud that, since *Night of the Solstice*, Blaine has always hired ghostwriters to write his books, but I can't prove that.

So I say, "If you want a list, I'll make a list."

"But that's not why I texted you earlier tonight. I texted you because you need to break up with Em."

"No problem," I say, even though, in my heart, a breakup is not happening. "We're not exactly lovey-dovey right now anyway."

"Good. Keep it that way."

"May I ask why?"

"Because we have dirt on her, bro."

"What kind?"

"Enough that she's risen on the Harn's suspect list."

"But what's the dirt?"

"She has a history of physical violence, Matt. Cuffed twice for assault. Both times involving women who were creative types. Both times released thanks to nolo contendere pleas to public intoxication, suggesting she had pricey legal advice, which all indications are she did."

"What do you mean, indications?"

"She's loaded, Matt. Her mother made it big in the art game;

ran with the Picasso-adulation crowd, got in early on buying
hundreds of sketches—Picasso sketched like a mad bastard,
you know—and there turned out to be mega money in that
down the line. And her father came from an oil family in Tex-
as. Worse, as far as her being a suspect, her parents divorced
because her father was a physically abusive philanderer, and
not long after they did, the father died suspiciously in a car
wreck. Brakes went out in the convertible he and his new young
girlfriend were driving down the Pacific Coast Highway. Nothing provable about who cut the brake-fluid line, but damned,
damned suspicious."

"Meaning what?"

"Meaning if the mother, who shortly thereafter offed herself with pills, didn't kill the guy, it's possible Em herself did."

"And Dawn thinks she's not done killing yet? How does this
explain the desire to kill female novelists?"

"Dawn doesn't have all the answers, bro. If she did, I'd be
talking to Em right now, not you."

I remember seeing a small sketch hanging in the foyer of
Em's apartment. I wondered if it was a Picasso then and now
figure it was. I remember Em sitting in the cab, craning her neck
to look out that window. So what if she killed her dad? I think.
So what?

"One point Dawn made was that Em's parents appear to
have been polar opposites who married each other for money,"
Jonas says. "Which is fine, of course, but it suggests she did
not have the happiest childhood. Still, they did sit on stacks of
cash, and she did put up with their lovelessness until they died,
so now she has those stacks."

"Do we know for a fact there was *always* lovelessness?" I ask.

"I suppose we don't for sure. But we know there was always
heavy drinking. Both of her parents were sieves. Which also
more or less explains her public intoxication pleas. Inability to
handle alcohol, of course, tends to run in families. Has she ever
had a few around you?"

No, I want to say.

But the Bureau might be all you have, I think.

"Matt?" Jonas says. "I asked you a question."

"She had some wine tonight," I say.

"Did her personality change?"

"Doesn't everyone's?"

"I take that as a yes."

I shrug.

"Did she seem volatile, Matt? Did she seem prone to anger and so forth?"

"Well, we did just have an argument."

"Then all the more reason."

"For what?"

"For you to keep away from her. You know, let the rest of us look into her."

"But that's not possible, Jonas."

"It'd better be possible. Because your standing orders from Harnischfeger are to stay away from her until Harnischfeger himself clears her."

"I meant it's not possible for her to have killed the four women."

"You're telling me she's not aggressive? Is she aggressive in bed?"

"That's none of your business."

"Fair enough. For now. Though this is the thing, bro: we were wrong about Hendee, so when it comes to this case going forward, we're trying to be more openminded."

"But I thought Trinko said there was a ninety-seven percent chance the Talent Killer is male."

"That's down to fifty-eight now. In part because of what I've turned up on Em. You gotta know, Matt, that I started out mostly trying to protect you two as a couple—I mean, I was trying to be your pal, so I just wanted to make sure there was no way she belonged on the list. But then things about her past just kept cropping up. Not to mention she was at the Cornelia when Jill Klugman read there."

"So you're saying you think she was envious of Jill."

"You tell me. Has she ever said anything to that effect?"

I remember Em praising Jill Klugman's story "Fiercely." I remember her asking my opinion of it. I realize maybe she'd hoped I'd say it was nothing special.

But no, I think.

No way can she be the Talent Killer.

"Not that I can recall," I say.

"Did she ever compare herself to other writers?" Jonas asks.

"Not really."

"Yes or no, Matt. This really is no time to be half-assed in your answers."

We walk on for about a block.

"Okay," I say. "She talked about other writers."

"Who?"

"Hendee for sure."

"What about female writers?"

"No," I say, well aware that I'm lying for her.

"You sure?" Jonas asks.

"Not that I can think of," I say, to give myself a small out.

"So can I be confident in taking from you that, far as you know, she never compared herself to other writers other than Hendee?"

"That's correct," I say.

Jonas says nothing as we walk several blocks. If he somehow knows I'm deceiving him, I think, he's using this silence to pressure me.

And I do feel this pressure, because I do love the Bureau.

Just tell him, I think.

Just tell him she went out of her way to find Jill's story and photocopy it and read it, and she probably wanted me to say it wasn't all it was cracked up to be. Just tell him that, yes, my heart is definitely with the Bureau, and, sure, she should probably be on the list.

But those bright eyes of Em's keep appearing in my mind. Bright from laughter. Bright from anger. Either way, they've taken hold of me, and, maybe worse, I don't mind that they have.

"So where does that leave us?" I ask Jonas as we walk on. We're hanging a right onto Tenth Avenue, the Hudson on our left, not a soul in sight for the few blocks we can see ahead.

"You mean where does that leave you and Em?"

"Yes."

"You need to keep clear of her, Matt. Can I ask why you and she had an argument tonight anyway?"

"It was my fault, really. She was flirting a little with Blaine, and that rubbed me the wrong way. It was one of those fights you have when you're drunk."

Jonas nods, considers this.

"In any event," he says, "from now on make it look like that was the end of the line for you. You've lost interest in her and are on toward other women. You're just another jerk out there who has fun with them but then makes it clear you'll never commit. In other words, you care more about yourself than you care about her."

But I *do* care about her, I think.

Lots.

"What if she phones me?" I ask.

"If she phones—or texts—maybe string her along for a while? So that maybe we can pick up on something about what she's been up to, what her mood is, who she's socializing with, and so on. But do it like a selfish prick in Manhattan would. You know, a shallow guy who just uses women for sex."

We walk on, Jonas and I.

Is this it? I wonder.

Is this conversation with Jonas how I break up with her?

Is this how it'll always be if you latch on to a permanent gig with the Bureau? No love with women? No simple love?

"Okay," I say.

"And remember, bro. The Bureau's listening in on both of your phones."

I nod, and Jonas assesses the lights on the other side of the
Hudson—New Jersey—as we continue walking uptown.
Dammit, I think.
Dammit.

16

I open an email from an unpublished writer. Like most I've read in the past week, it offers a parade of clichéd phrases, subject-verb agreement problems, and an obtuseness with punctuation that assures me texting is indeed the end of literature. Worse, no writer contacting me so far has portrayed the anger Harnischfeger wants.

Then, though, I'm reading a sample chapter that won't allow me to click it away.

Even before I finish it, I tap the JONAS icon on my phone.

"Yes, Matt."

"I might have one here."

"Erratically written?"

"Yes."

"Violent?"

"Very."

"Sick and twisted violence?"

"Well, brother, you tell me. Opening chapter's from the point of view of a guy who envies a woman because the woman is a better dancer. Guy visits the woman at three a.m. under the guise of being depressed because he's unsuccessful professionally speaking—tells her he needs the shoulder of another dancer to cry on. He supposedly charms her with some stilted dialogue, excuses himself from her living room couch to go use the can, only he doesn't use the can. He goes into her kitchen."

"And gets, what, a butcher knife?"

"A steak knife. He looks for a butcher knife, can't find one—which, to this author's credit, did make for a few decent lines of suspense."

"Curious."

"Why curious?"

"Arguably an admission and a denial at the same time."

"How do you mean?"

"To the author's having used a butcher knife on the four victims."

"I see."

"Classic sociopath, I'm guessing Trinko would say. Did the guy do authoritative work cutting her up?"

"Stabbed her midsection first to get her to recoil, then went straight for the jugular."

"Uh-huh. Any verbal expressions of anger?"

"None said aloud, but quite a few thought."

"Like stream-of-consciousness thoughts?"

"Yep. Your basic workshoppy, run-on-sentence stuff, only a helluva lot angrier."

"How about typos? Lots?"

"Yes."

"Proliferating where the anger peaked?"

"Yes, and the thing is, I never get the willies reading sample chapters of blood and gore, but this time, I did. I mean, the guy then goes out and buys four bottles of bleach to clean up. I mean, who'd think to go with *four* gallons—unless he himself had stabbed and dismembered someone and used four?"

"Okay, forward it. I'll look it over and let Harn take a gander if I see fit. We're still pretty deep into looking into some other leads here, so I'll let you know if we'll need you to follow up."

"So, wait—shouldn't this pretty much knock Em off the list?"

"I'm saying don't respond to this guy until someone from the Bureau tells you to. It was a guy who sent the query, right?"

"Androgynous first name, so I'm not sure."

"What name is that?"

"Brett."

"Last name?"

"Smith."

"That's not a very creative writer. Forward it, pal."

And with that, Jonas hangs up.

I'm holding my breath, I realize. I allow an exhale. This is your job, I think. Grunt work. I forward Brett Smith's email and the phone rings: EM. Aware that someone at the Bureau is probably listening in, I don't answer—to protect her. The phone keeps ringing.

Of course, I miss her. Our argument in the cab now has me more curious about what she was thinking while she looked out that window. Was she thinking about her father? Her mother? Could she really have killed her father? I need to talk to her. I tell myself I could do her a favor by getting her to say something that'll convince Harnischfeger to scratch her off the list. I realize I'm rationalizing, but I don't care.

I answer and say, "Hi!"—maybe too cheerfully.

"Hi!" she says as if she's never suspected me of a thing.

"What's up?" I ask. I realize I'm looking down at the silver roof next door.

"The struggle. You?"

"Working. Sorry I haven't called. It's just that I've been so—"

"Listen, Matt. I'm kind of uncomfortable with small talk right now. There's something big I need to tell you."

No, I think, but with the Bureau likely in on the call, I can't say No. *Integrity*, I think, and I ask, "What is it?"

"It's about something that happened the other night."

"Oh?"

"When we were at Blaine's place. It's something that came up between me and Lauren when she showed me where the bathroom was."

"Uh-huh?" I say, and I remember Lauren flirting with Considine way back when, my breaths all at once shallow, my face hot.

"It's something you might not exactly enjoy hearing, so, I don't know, maybe take a Valium or something?"

"I'll be fine. Remember, I lived with convicts twenty-four seven for years. How bad can anything else be?"

Em says nothing. I step into the bathroom, look at myself in the mirror, dislike the pallor I see, leave the bathroom and stand in the middle of the main room, facing the television, then the bed, then the ceiling, then the bed.

Em says, "What happened was…Lauren kind of…opened up to me."

I wait to hear more.

I consider clicking on the TV but don't.

"About what?" I ask.

"About something very…you know, secret about herself."

Lauren killed the four women? I think.

No, I think. "What did she tell you?" I ask.

"Matt, this isn't easy for me to say."

"Just lay it out, Em. I'm a big boy."

"Lauren…"

"Yes?"

"She never did it with Consee, Matt."

"*What?*"

"She never cheated on you with Consee. You know, the guy you…you know, strangled."

"Yes, I know who we mean by Consee—"

"She never had sex with him, Matt."

"But—"

"She did it with Blaine. I mean, back then. I mean, back when Blaine told you Consee was sleeping with her, it was Blaine himself who was actually sleeping with her."

My face must be crimson, given how it feels. I can muster only the words, "No shit?"

"God's honest truth."

For a moment or two, I can't hear. I need to swallow, but my throat's stuck, though I'm salivating severely, and the hand I'm using to hold the phone has gone slick.

"Just to make sure I heard you right," I say. "You're telling me *Blaine* was the one who was having the affair with Lauren?"

"Yes."

"The only one."

"Yes."

"You're saying Consee never slept with her once."

"Correct."

"So when Blaine told me Consee was sleeping with her, he was bullshitting me."

"Yup."

"Are you sure?"

"This is what Lauren told me. Why would she tell me that—and all these years later—if it weren't true?"

"So when I ran over to Consee's place all ticked off, it was because…it was because…it was because Blaine had set me up to think Consee was fucking her so I wouldn't suspect Blaine himself was."

"Yes."

"Meaning I killed Consee for no reason."

"Apparently."

"Why didn't you tell me this sooner?"

"I wanted to in the cab after we left their stupid penthouse. But you were—well, I was scared about how you'd react."

My mind spins off. There's not one thought I can hold onto. It feels as if deceit's everywhere in the world. I know this is impossible, but I feel it as the truth nonetheless. I can't breathe and now I'm faint, my lungs feeling as if they're being punctured by hundreds of pins.

Then I hear Em saying, "…she was pretty upset, Matt. She was drunk but coherent, and really upset. I think that her seeing you in the flesh after all those years…"

My head hurts. My neck, the insides of my arms, my palms, my fingertips. Heart attack, I think, so I stand and take deep breaths while holding one arm, then the other, over my head.

I manage to say, "So you're saying she was ideally drunk for truth-telling."

"Yes. Because she also spilled the beans about how things have been going lately between her and Blaine."

"Oh?"

"Lots of tension between them, Matt. Lots of drinking and arguing."

"Did she say what about?"

"Not directly. She did mention that she hates how other women throw themselves at him. Apparently sometimes she just goes off on him. She said they were arguing the other night about a letter he got from some hottie who claimed to be his 'most ardent' fan, and she—Lauren—told him you're a better writer than he is. Apparently this really set him off."

I'm trembling inside. I'm dizzy, my teeth all but chattering.

"Gonna go now, Em," I say.

"Okay, but remember I'm here?"

"Right," I say, and I hang up and take the deepest breath possible.

But I'm still trembling. Teeth clenched, I walk over to the window. The workers are on the roof, teamed up on some task. One of them glances over, then goes on ignoring me like the rest.

The phone rings.

Jonas.

Using his personal number.

"Yeah," I say.

"You okay?"

"Why wouldn't I be?"

"I just heard. I was listening in."

"Well, what are you gonna do, right? It's not like no one else in the world has ever been cheated on."

"I guess."

"Is Harnischfeger on the line?"

"He's having lunch, so it's possible he's not at the moment. But hey, just wanted to say I'm sorry to have heard about this. Man-to-man, friend-to-friend—whatever you want to call it."

"Yeah, well. I knew Lauren was being bopped by *someone* back then."

"Yes, but, Matt—you killed the wrong guy."

"Thanks for being such a pal by rubbing that in."

"I didn't mean to—"

"Can we just forget it? Either way, Lauren didn't love me. I mean, okay, yeah, I spent four-plus years behind bars for a pointless crime, but there's a Talent Killer out there, so let's get back to finding him."

"Or her," Jonas says.

"You're saying you still suspect Em?"

"The Harn does, so I do too. Hang on, Matt, I'm gonna patch in Trinko. If you don't mind?"

"Not at all," I say, much as I'm overwhelmed. Rage, disappointment, embarrassment—I'm embodying all these lovelies.

Then I hear a woman's voice say, "Matt?"

"Dawn?" I say.

"Yessir."

"I'm still here also," Jonas says. "Go ahead, Trinko."

"Listen, Matt," Trinko says. "We want to update you a little on some details about your friend Em. A few things you probably hadn't quite known about."

"Of course."

"You sure you're okay with hearing about her now?"

"Why wouldn't I be?"

"Well, we all know about your call with her just now."

"Yeah, well, I'm fine. That marriage has been over for years—I'm fine."

"Okay then," Trinko says. "In the past few days, Em's been emailing herself notes about you. And we're not quite sure why. A few of us think she's keeping a diary of sorts, and that she's doing this with emails because she doesn't trust that her laptop won't crash."

"Uh-huh."

"Anyway in one of these entries, she mentioned that you told her you wrote *Night of the Solstice* for Blaine Davis."

"Uh-huh."

"Is this true?"

"You mean is it true that I told her I wrote it, or that I wrote it?"

"Both."

"I did write it—I mean, I rewrote almost all of it pretty much from scratch—and, yes, I told her so."

"And I take it you understand why this matters to the Bureau, correct?"

"Actually, I don't."

Trinko goes silent, apparently choosing her words.

Jonas clears his throat loudly and says, "Matty. Em's still a person of interest, at the very least. So just use common sense from there, bro. Her knowledge of you being the actual author of *Night of the Solstice* gives her significant reason to envy you."

"Right," I say, and I remember Em in bed with me after we met in the old diner on Duane, kissing my mouth gently while lying on top of me.

"Was that a sarcastic *right*, Matt?" Trinko asks.

"Maybe a little," I say.

"Listen, Matt," Jonas says. "Here's the deal. Believe what you want personally, but if you have any plans whatsoever to work undercover with the Bureau rather than go back upstate, stay more than seventy-five feet away from that woman."

"Okay."

"You mean that seriously, Matt?" Trinko asks.

"Yes," I say.

"And here," Jonas says. "Just got an email from the Harn telling me that the query you sent us—from that Brett Smith person—struck him as suspicious enough that he wants to check the guy out."

"He just now forwarded that query to me," Trinko says. "I'm off now to give it a look."

And with that, the connection between me and the Bureau goes dead, my mouth ajar. I'm still facing the silver roof. The men who were on it are gone. Only now does it begin to seep in to the point that I feel it, concern about what Em's passion in bed has been all about.

I check my phone for anything from her. Nothing, from her or from anyone. I'm hungry. I leave the apartment in search of a bodega, find one two blocks uptown and four west. I buy a pre-wrapped chicken with pesto sandwich, manage to get it down.

Back in the apartment, I read my new emails. Only a few more have come in: one from a woman in Oregon, another from a guy in Utah, a third from a self-proclaimed "divorcee" in Madison, Wisconsin, who has attached two files, her sample chapter and a selfie of her in red panties and nothing else.

I focus on her smile only—all I want is Em.

Another email pings in. It's from Blaine Davis, a single sentence presented in one of the offbeat fonts he apparently still likes to play with: Attached is a little bit of it, in case you've realized my current offer ($200,000) could do you and your new woman some good.

I open the attachment:

"What can I help you with?" she asked.

You tell me, he wanted to say.

But no, he thought. Talking sexy too soon would blow everything.

"I'm a friend of your husband's," he said. "Did he tell you I saw him last night? At a bar?"

"No," she said. "What are you...I mean—I'm sorry—where did you see him?"

And back went one of her bare feet. No paint on the toenails but back went the other, back toward the living room, back to where her coffee waited, to where this bungalow she lived in harbored more heat than this 7:00 a.m. chill he and she endured for the time being. Back to where no neighbors could see.

"Come in," she said, which, to him, meant she wanted one thing only: to hear about what he knew her husband had done last night.

And there he was, inside. Once you were in, you had them. Unless, of course, you then went for it too soon. His face, from what he could feel of it despite his meds, was trying its best for innocuous.

She said, "I suppose I should ask you to have a seat."

"Appreciate it," he said, and he forewent the

chintz-covered chair to sit on the middle of the plaid couch. She remained standing, facing him directly, her chest slightly thrust against her sweater's fabric—already wanting his touch? She hadn't yet asked him his name and that was an excellent sign. She'd craved this couch, he believed, back when she and her husband had first seen it online, so don't push too fast, he thought. Her husband. Her husband. He couldn't stop thinking about her husband. His thumb flicked piping along the edge of a cushion as he said, "Your husband didn't mention he saw me?"

"Saw you when?"

"Last night."

"No. In fact he said nothing about being at a bar."

"That's odd," he said, and he thought: doable.

"Why is that odd?" she asked.

"Well, maybe it's not. I was just thinking that if you and your husband had a close relationship, then..."

She didn't appear nervous, which, given the others, could cut either way.

"Then...what?" this one said.

"Then I'd think he would have mentioned having— you know—seen me in the bar."

And he knew very well to sit wordlessly now.

Just sit.

As if no adult in the world ever thought about sex.

"Would you maybe like some coffee?" she asked.

Bingo, he thought.

"That could be splendid," he said, his enunciation slightly off. "That is," he added, "if what you have is hot."

She might have smiled a little. But he knew again to go quiet. And to ignore the swaying of her breasts as she crossed the room to head for the kitchen.

The ass, of course, being another matter.

"I mean as long as—" he called. Machiavelli, he

thought. Praise her and make every move like Machia-velli would. "I mean as long as you don't end up feeling too put out," he heard himself saying, and once it started, it always went like this, his volume difficult to gauge, his physical self, clean or not, charged all the more by his pulse. He was even more aroused on his way into the kitchen, a half-empty coffee mug—the dumb-shit hus-band's?—on the table, and she had a cabinet open, her torso and arms and neck reaching high, her toes strained as she rose higher still, her black yoga pants proving she took pride in her looks.

She took her time as she continued to reach. She was playing both angelic and seductive while presumably flummoxed in search of a third mug, he thought.

Just touch her, he thought.

Just let her know what you want.

Just show her how a man without a wife does it.

And that's the end of the attachment. For Blaine, decent on the line level—the result of line-editing he paid for, no doubt. So the quality of the writing itself isn't why his satisfaction clause money is being withheld. It's being withheld because his publisher thinks he's a perv.

And I have to agree with her: how else could he have come up with this chapter? I've long known, given my experience as his agent, that his fiction is autobiographical. And I now know that, in his personal experience, he seduced and stole at least one wife: Lauren.

He gets off on ruining love, I think.

That's why all the flirting with Em the other night.

I raise my phone, find the JONAS icon, tap it.

"Yeah?" Jonas says.

"Hey, got another interesting email here."

"Oh?"

"From Blaine Davis. He wants me to rewrite his next book because his publisher won't pay him until he redoes it."

"So?"

"So he sent a writing sample, and it suggests he's an extremely sick womanizer who grooves on sending relationships down the tubes."

"So?"

"So I think he belongs on the list."

Jonas grants me a few moments of apparent consideration.

Then: "Matt, here's the thing. The Talent Killer's motive has nothing to do with sexual desire. Or even a desire to—as you put it—send relationships down the tubes. It's just plain envy of talent, bro, literary talent. And that's why your friend Em is rising on the list. In fact, I just found even more on her. Turns out she's a failed novelist, not the memoirist she told you she was when you first met her at the Cornelia Café, and she's been revising the same novel for years—*and* queried every agent under the sun with numerous drafts, with each draft being rejected by everyone."

"Then why hasn't she ever queried me?"

"She has, Matt. Since you're on the payroll, we've taken the liberty of checking your emails from when you were doing time, and there they were, four different queries from her regarding this same manuscript of hers. Each using a different title, presumably with a revised draft."

"So what are you saying?"

"I'm saying she's apparently less and less like the person you've been thinking she is."

"Okay. Point taken. But isn't that what people do? Fib a little when they start dating someone?"

"Maybe so, Matt. And I realize it probably seems to you like there's no way she could do you harm. But you have to remember that a good chunk of homicides happen between people who started out, at one point in time, liking each other. So even if she's falling in *love* with you, bro, that doesn't do much to save your hide. Because what matters foremost is motive, and when it comes to you, she now appears to have motive to spare. In any case, she's a frustrated novelist with multiple arrests for assaulting creative types, who's been misleading you about who she really is, and whose prose strikes Dawn as gratuitously violent. Prose which, by the way, narrates at decent length the process of a female character's cutting the brake fluid line of a man she once had fondness for."

I go tongue-tied.

Okay, I want to say, but I can't.

"So the chances of her going after you are now higher, so we have to make sure she lacks opportunity," Jonas says. "From the Bureau's point of view, it's as simple as that."

"Even though she likes me, huh," I say, somewhat kiddingly, and Jonas goes quiet, maybe to smile, maybe to shake his head, or, maybe, I realize, to wince.

17

The queries continue to flow in. Easily one per minute in my email account, sometimes a barrage of far more. Many are from short story writers, poets with one or two online credits at most, PhDs who seem to have rarely stepped off their college campuses, or "life coaches" whose manuscripts are titled *You Be You* or words to that effect. Nothing smacks of a seven-figure deal, or, for that matter, of any deal. I'm not sure which is causing me to feel edgier by the hour: my desire to catch the Talent Killer or my need to latch on as a lifer with the Bureau.

But no writing sample that implies a homicidal, frustrated writer is coming my way. The closest to suspicious are chapters of novels in which women *want* to kill their abusive husbands but then leave them for professors of the softer sciences (sociology, psychology, and, more often than anything, anthropology) who whisk them off to Europe, where they engage in dialogue of little consequence. No tension to speak of once they meet Mr. Right. No motivation to kill.

Then, minutes after I consider leaving Manhattan for a job selling real estate, my phone vibrates more loudly than usual.

DAWN.

I answer with a professional sounding "Yes?"

"Is this Matt?"

"It is. Did you just make my phone vibrate louder than usual?"

"I did. And I'm a little pressed for time, Matt, so I'd prefer to get right to what I'm calling about—your theory that your pal Blaine Davis should be on the list?"

"Sure. What do you think? Didn't that sample of his kind of creep you out?"

"Crumple and toss."

"Pardon?"

"Bureau-speak for forget about it."

"Seriously?"

"Yes."

"May I ask why?"

"If you don't mind my being direct: you're just jealous of the guy."

"But I don't think I am."

"But you just found out that he slept with Lauren when you were married to her and, presumably, loved her."

"Presumably."

"Well, did you love her back then or not?"

I go quiet, remembering my marriage, remembering even more fondly Lauren and me before our marriage. How, for me, it was love at first sight, how our first kiss struck me as irreplaceable one moment in.

"These past twenty-four hours haven't been easy on you, Matt," Dawn continues. "You learned you did time for killing the wrong person. You learned the man who stole your wife took her from you long before you found out, and was a conniver you'd made rich and famous by doing his literary grunt work. You learned the woman you now have a thing for might be a serial killer. And, as the kicker, that this woman, this new one, might happen to want to kill and dismember you."

I close my eyes to try to slow down my mind. I picture Lauren and me dressed to the nines on the day we got married and think: *You don't love her.* Nor do you love *her*, I think while picturing Em wrapped in her comforter on her designer couch. You don't love or need anyone, I tell myself, and I promise myself everything's fine.

"Okay," I say. "My last seventy-two hours or so haven't exactly been a walk in the park, but that doesn't mean Blaine isn't a sick and twisted perv who's been killing talented writers."

"That's your opinion, Matt."

"You're saying no one at the Bureau agrees with me?"

"Correct."

"Harnischfeger included."

"That's right. And Harnischfeger and the Bureau as a whole need you to accept that you have personal biases against Blaine and in favor of Em. Biases you've got to get over, Matt. You've got to let them go so you can do your best work for us."

"But I am doing my best work."

"But I haven't seen a violent writing sample for days."

"Because since the one from Blaine, I haven't received any."

"Not *one*?"

"That's correct. Maybe you didn't realize this, Dawn, but generally speaking? The product of the typical aspiring writer is pretty goddamned tame."

Dawn goes quiet and stays that way.

I've convinced her? I think.

She believes I still belong on the case?

"Well, stay on it," she finally says. "Do all you can to keep your emotions at bay, and keep on reading those emails."

18

A nd I do keep on reading them. I am one with my phone, eating with it, sleeping with it, watching it as it sits on the bathroom sink while I brush my teeth.

And starting the next morning, it does connect me to people of interest—but of interest only to me in my capacity as a literary agent. Acquiring editors from various houses overseas make offers for Hendee's collection of poems and forthcoming novel. Film people are dangling options. I even receive a couple offers for books written by other clients I represented before my arrest, offers that would make any literary agent feel almost loved.

I go on, in the several days that follow, to make numerous deals, most of them for Hendee. A signed film contract leads to a celebratory dinner uptown enjoyed by Hendee and me and Doreen, including shots of tequila insisted upon by Doreen, lots of laughter on her and Hendee's part, and a sense of wonderment I haven't observed in years.

I also of course continue to read queries as they pour in. The deals I made for Hendee have really opened the spigots— queries are popping up left and right. Given how many aspiring writers exist in the world, and how stealthy the Talent Killer continues to prove to be, I feel buried by work.

Then comes an email from Em. In its memo line are nothing but three consecutive question marks. It's 1:30 p.m., I realize. Independent wealth translates to boredom, which translates to wanting to see me?

My racing heart assures me I still have it bad for her.

Then I see the only line of the email:

Pls tell me it wasn't Hendee.

No-no-no, please no, I think. Even before I find the remote, I'm rubber-legged. I go so light-headed I sit on the bed, where

I can't stop my thumb as it clicks from one channel to the next.

Then, in crawlers easing across the bottom of the screen, are words that stop my mind cold:

...a portion of a fifth victim has been found...

...by a dogwalker in Manhattan's Riverside Park...

...the FBI confirms that this time...

...the victim was male...

I shudder. *No*, I keep thinking, but I'm standing and pacing without remembering when I first stood.

I try closing my eyes, breathing through my nostrils only—all the tricks. It occurs to me to do what any rational person in my position should do, call Hendee.

And at first I can't.

Then, despite myself, I'm doing it.

Then I'm hearing his phone ring and ring, and, finally, go to voicemail.

"Hend, give me a call, buddy," I say, but my voice betrays that I fear there will never be such a call.

I redial repeatedly, hear nothing but ringing. I leave the apartment. Remain upright on Duane despite serious vertigo. Avoid hailing the first cab I see because I can't bear the thought of interacting with a human being. Then I'm hailing one, and then I'm in it, closing the door. "Mott and Canal," I am saying in a voice that doesn't sound much at all like my own.

I can't handle the sight of myself in the rearview mirror. Jonas isn't calling, I realize, and I try to take this as a good sign, but it's not a good sign, my jittery, truth-hungry mind finally forces me to admit. Jonas might simply be waiting for me to learn on my own—he doesn't want to be the one to break the news to me personally.

I want to call Em, but what if she's the killer? She *was* envious of Hendee; she definitely knew how much I admired him and his work. She couldn't not know how talented he was, and she'd known longer than anyone but me and him that he'd recently been offered all kinds of deals. She probably despised him more than the typical twenty-year-old writer did—no one writes and rewrites books and hounds agents for years unsuccessfully without coming apart inside at least a little.

She killed him, I think.

She killed all of them.

The cab pulls over, brakes.

He's fine, I try to tell myself.

The odds say he's at his laptop and writing a poem, right?

There are dozens of male writers in this city who could've been sliced up.

I calm myself enough that my legs leave the cab.

I'm trembling inside, but I'm walking.

Then I'm in the shaded alleyway behind Hendee's building. I see that the horizontal door leading to the basement is down and shut. I grow close enough to it to notice that it's locked.

Because Hendee himself locked it, I think.

Because he's out buying fried dumplings.

"Matt?" I hear, from the entrance to the alleyway behind me. I glance over my shoulder and see Doreen, and the look on her face says she's beyond worried. There are words coming out of her mouth, but they're not registering in me, maybe because she's speaking too softly, maybe because the whirring in my mind has overcome my hearing. I do hear myself saying *What?*—and, now that she's standing closer to me, I hear her say she hasn't seen him or heard from him for days.

My fists, I realize, are clenched.

"That doesn't mean anything," I say.

"Then where is he?" she asks.

"He could be anywhere," I say as calmly as I can. "I'm sure he's fine."

"But where *is* he?"

"He's always been like that. You know, unpredictable."

But in fact, Ethan Hendee has never been unpredictable. I've never known him not to be down there, in his tiny hovel of an apartment, writing unpunctuated poems.

I feel my hand vibrate—my phone.

JONAS.

Doreen, slack-jawed, watches me.

I tap the correct icon, manage to say, "Yes?"

"Matty," Jonas's voice says, and it's because of his tone that I know.

But I realize that, to assure I remain undercover, I can't tell Doreen what I know—because if the Bureau is hours or days away from making Hendee's identity public, who'd be calling me now to let me know it was him?

"I'm sorry, Matt," Jonas says. "More than I can express."

I go dizzy. I lean against Hendee's building to steady myself. I click off the phone, gaze down at the padlock on the horizontal door. Someone other than Hendee locked it, I realize—which means if Doreen has the key to the padlock, she very well could be the killer.

"Do you have the key?" I ask her.

She's crying. She appears devastated. She shakes her head no, and I believe her. I tell myself not to trust her, but my gut tells me to believe her.

"Who was that calling you?" she asks.

"Someone else in publishing," I say, "who's as worried about him as we are."

"Have they heard from him at all?"

"No."

My phone rings again. It's Em.

I answer with a "Hi."

"Checking in to see how you're doing," she says.

"Thanks."

"Where are you?"

"At Hendee's place. With Doreen."

"Did you guys hear?"

"That they found the male victim?" I ask.

"That they identified him as Hendee."

Doreen is watching me closely, hanging on my every word, so I keep things vague by saying, "Okay."

"Try to latch onto a bright thought, Matt," Em says. "The Ferrari brain's gonna kick in now, so try to slow it down."

But already I'm picturing Em visiting Hendee in his tiny place, inviting him to hers, seducing him, stabbing him, poisoning him—doing whatever she does if she's the Talent Killer.

And she *is* the Talent Killer, I think. And she knows I'm undercover—she's known since she first saw me posing with Jonas at the Cornelia.

"Matt?" she's saying now, through the phone.

"Yes?" I answer.

"It's happening, right? In your mind?"

Doreen is wide-eyed, still watching me.

"Here," I say to Em. "Talk to Doreen. She needs you to tell her everything you know."

19

The longer I walk uptown on Mott, the more despondent I grow. I dislike the pedestrians coming at me. Most everyone, in my mind, is guilty of murder, adultery, tax fraud, *some* crime deserving time behind bars or worse. I'm glaring at people. I cannot bear the sight of them. Their heads, their torsos, their legs, their feet—they are all such heaps of imperfection, and, worse, they strike me as full of themselves, cutthroat, determined to do whatever it takes to serve themselves first before doing so much as a favor for anyone else. My head hurts. I don't know what to do with my hands. Now and then I want to grab someone, usually a middle-aged man, by the shoulders and scream all manner of curse words at him.

I manage to press on, keeping my thoughts to myself.

Just after I lock myself into the apartment on Duane, I receive a text from Harnischfeger. I do not read it immediately. I lie on the bed, close my eyes, take a deep breath through my nose, let it out through my mouth.

He's gone, I think.

He wrote all those poems, and you failed him, and he's gone.

Then I think: *Fidelity, Bravery, Integrity.*

What else do you have left?

I tap Harnischfeger's text up onto my screen:

Meet me @ the Ramble @ 4p today in the small meadow east of the hanging bird feeders beside the snaking dirt path through the woods.

Alone.

I check the time: 2:23.

I know the Ramble's in Central Park, but I don't know precisely where. I google it: southern half of the park, near the Loeb Boathouse.

You can walk that and make it, I think.

You need to walk it to calm yourself.

Just don't let your eyes meet anyone's.

I text Harnischfeger back with *Will do.* Google "small meadow in Ramble" to be sure Harnischfeger and I are of the same mind. Find a photo of it, ask Google for walking directions. Leave the apartment, head uptown, manage to avoid eye contact with most of the people walking toward me. Two clip my elbow with theirs, one as if intent on jarring me, but rather than cussing I think *Justice* and remain on course.

Then I'm in the park, dealing primarily with joggers. A bike zips past. The sight of a gondola near the shore of the pond beside the Loeb Boathouse calms me but only temporarily.

Then I'm in it, the Ramble. As per online, birds abound. I find the dirt path, the bird feeders, the small meadow, which I cross to sit on the one concrete bench. Birds are chirping to beat hell.

Harnischfeger emerges from between tree trunks and begins toward me. No Jonas with him, no Trinko—it's just us. The birds keep on with their din, and he stops within three feet of me, remains standing while looking down at me.

"You doin' all right?" he asks, his gray-blue eyes those of a sleep-deprived pro.

"Yessir."

"It would be natural for you to need time to recover emotionally."

"Time before what?"

"You continue on."

"With the investigation?"

"Yes."

"I'm fine," I say. "Look." I hold out a hand, palm up. It's steady. Harnischfeger studies it suspiciously, so I hold out the other. It's steady as well, which, if I'm honest with myself, surprises me.

He nods but looks off, perturbed by something, maybe the persistent birdsong. Lets his weary eyes return to mine. In them is need. "I'm concerned about Jonas," he says barely louder than the birds.

"Oh?"

He cocks his head slightly, as if doubting whether we should be talking.

"A few of his colleagues at headquarters," he says, "including Trinko, have come to me. And Trinko's worried because he's been...well, there's only one way to put this, Matt, odd as it might sound: people have seen verses on scraps of paper on his desk."

"Verses?"

"He's writing poems, Matt."

Now it's my turn to hesitate. "Maybe I'm missing something here," I say carefully, "but are Jonas's hobbies our biggest concern?"

He readjusts his hands on his hips. Looks off again, this time to watch a woman pushing a stroller on the path beyond the meadow, glancing at us innocuously, then continuing on the path as it reenters the woods.

"Matt," he finally says, "the writing of quatrains and so forth has never exactly been a pastime I like to see UC people engage in."

"Because it's a distraction?"

"Not so much that. More so because it's a sign of not being able to handle the pressure. Not to mention if Jonas aspires to write and publish poetry, I need to—as head of this investigation—address the possibility that he himself might've been envious of Hendee."

I recall Jonas showing me his poem on the Staten Island Ferry, then asking me not to tell anyone in the Bureau about it. I realize that he seemed dead set on putting Hendee behind bars from the moment we met on that hoop court in the yard in Sing Sing.

"So now *Jonas* is a suspect," I say.

"If he's seriously into poetry, Matt, he could be. And at this point, I'm not willing to rule anyone out. You need to remember, this poetry business is something I know basically nothing about, and we got too many dead bodies."

My mind's off and running. If I mention the poem Jonas tried to show me on the ferry, he'll rise on Harnischfeger's list. If I don't, I might be protecting the Talent Killer.

"Well?" Harnischfeger says. "Jonas has spent a decent amount of time with you. Anything about him you'd like to share?"

No way, I think. No way would Jonas do anyone harm.

Then I remember Lauren's cheating and remind myself I'm not the best judge of character.

Still, I am saying, "In my opinion, sir, a few stanzas on a desk mean nothing."

"What if I told you he ordered some poetry books online?"

"I guess I'd ask if you were just raising a hypothetical question or—"

"He ordered some, Matt. He's been buying those kinds of books for years now, sixteen all told. To me, that's not exactly proof that he's heavily into writing the stuff, but I'm no expert on how people become poets. So, well, that's why I'm asking my expert in that field—you—if you've sensed, or you flat-out know, that in fact he has any aspirations of that sort."

I remember my outburst of anger on the ferry. *He wanted you to represent him*, I think despite myself. *He wanted to be the next Hendee*. But now that Hendee is dead, Jonas is the closest thing I have to a pal, and I don't want to rat out a pal.

My compromise of sorts is to try to answer Harnischfeger with my facial expression:

Yes, that makes Jonas a poet, is what my eyes and arched eyebrows try to say. *Yes, much as I hate to say it, he probably should be on our suspect list.*

And Harnischfeger seems to get this, because he recoils physically. Only a fraction of an inch, but still.

"Okay," he says. "Okay."

So that's it, I think. You haven't squealed explicitly, but you and the Bureau are square.

"So who's going to wire me up before Hendee's funeral?" I ask. "I assume not him."

"I don't know. I need to bring him in and sit him down."

"Of course."

"In any event, stay put in the apartment the morning of the funeral until someone with a badge stops by."

"What morning will that be?"

"Day after tomorrow. That is, if Hendee's sister can get it arranged in time."

"Hendee had a sister?"

"Yes."

"I had no idea."

"I'm guessing because she's a nun? He and she lost touch after their brother died, both kind of going their own ways, she to a convent in western Pennsylvania, he to Chinatown. Her name's Marnie."

"Is she a suspect?"

"No more than anyone else."

I find myself missing Em badly. Maybe I don't have what it takes to work for the Bureau? Maybe I'm a hopeless romantic?

The birds chirp on, maybe flirting, maybe arguing. I clear my throat. "Can I ask you something?" I say.

"Of course," Harnischfeger says.

"After I'm wired for the funeral, I'm free?"

"What do you mean?"

"To interact with everyone there including Em?"

Harnischfeger regards me more closely. Obviously he knows a smitten man when he sees one.

"No physical contact of any kind," he says. "Until you know she's off the list."

I nod.

He looks down at his chest, reaches inside his jacket, takes out his phone, taps it and holds it to his ear. "Yes?"

He listens to whomever as I listen to the birds.

"Of course," he says into the phone, and he taps off the call. "Anything else we need to go over?" he asks me.

"Just one more question."

"Sure."

"What if Jonas calls me between now and the funeral?"

"Don't answer. Till the funeral, you're all about reading those queries. I assume plenty are still coming in?"

I nod.

"Good. Stay on them. And forward anything suspicious to Dawn rather than Jonas. Because who knows, tonight you might receive the one that counts. Listen, there's someone I need to meet downtown in half an hour. You need anything else?"

"No. We're good."

And with that, Harnischfeger turns and makes his way across the meadow and hangs a left onto the narrow dirt path.

And I'm struck with the realization that I might never see him again—or, for that matter, Jonas.

Because *someone* else you know is going to end up face-to-face with the killer, I think.

I absorb the birdsong as the truth of this sinks in. I consider the likelihood, the solid likelihood, that the Talent Killer is Em, not Jonas. I give reason a good chance in me, allow it to permeate me best it can, but then, nonetheless, I doubt that she could hurt anyone. The passion of hers I've known—it's felt too much like love.

I realize there's a part of me that doesn't give a damn that, objectively, in the eyes of the Bureau, the chances of her being the killer are greater than I want them to be. I don't want Jonas to be the killer either, but if he is, he is—so be it.

I stand and walk toward the narrow path. I try not to think about Hendee as I head back downtown.

And by the time I reach Forty-Seventh or so, I'm able to cross paths with people without feeling any animosity whatsoever.

I'm better now.

I'm the me who gets along.

I believe I have Em to thank for this.

Back in the apartment on Duane, I open my email account to read queries. Two hundred thirty-seven have arrived since I last checked, and two more pop up before I settle in to read. I haven't eaten since breakfast but am not hungry in the least. I pore over about three dozen queries before I come upon a live one. Crime novel by someone going by the name Richard Bowers, no publication credits, Brooklyn Heights address. The pitch line he's offered in his opening paragraph: "I hope you'll represent *Next*, my suspense novel about a seemingly unstoppable spree of murders occurring in a major metropolitan area that baffles even the most experienced homicide detectives in the FBI."

Okay, Richard, I think as I open his sample chapters. There are three. The first is from the point of view of a detective most recently assigned to the case, a forty-ish, well-read divorced guy who, bam, has a head of white hair.

Relax, I think. Probably coincidence.

But the second chapter is from the point of view of a woman who, as I read her, may or may not be the killer: buoyant and attractive on the outside, depressed and angry otherwise.

Not Em—not really, I think, but I shiver.

Then there's a third chapter, from the point of view of a twenty-four-year-old man who graduated from Bard with a BA in English but is now a hunting guide—professionally. He lives alone and keeps dozens of hunting knives, as well as butcher knives in his kitchen, which is tricked out with a stainless-steel table for butchering the squirrels, rabbits, wild turkeys, and deer he and his clients have shot upstate. He spends hours on end playing the same game on his phone, in which all manner of people on city streets can be chased down by a clown who changes color from purple to blue to green to yellow to neon pink depending on its speed. You make the clown either male or female by one click of a button, even in the middle of a chase. You start playing by typing in the name of the NYC borough you want the clown to wake up in, then the first name of the person you want him to stalk, then the name of the street you want him to begin stalking them on and whether you want him to head north, south, east, or west. You do not click icons to give directions. You need to type directions as imperative sentences, and if you spell incorrectly, you lose ground on the person you intend to kill. The longer you spell correctly, the faster you go. It strikes me as implausible as a game people would play on their phones, but then again, I've been away for more than four years—and, well, reading about the professional hunter's obsession with the game causes me to break out in a sweat.

In the email in which I forward the query to Trinko, I type only this:

Am I crazy or is this TTK?

I watch my phone, waiting for her response. I realize she's busy but keep staring.

This is it, I think.

This guy's going to the top of the list.

I lie on the bed and continue to watch the screen. I'm exhausted, I realize. Other emails ping in but I don't care. I'm not hungry, though I'm weak and trembling on and off, so I head out of the building and west on Duane for the bodega, where I buy three power bars and a bottle of seltzer. I'm able to eat a power bar on the first block of my walk home, but the trembling grows worse. My phone's not ringing, pinging, vibrating—nothing. I consider that it's possible Jonas is the Talent Killer and is so twisted he posed as this guy in Brooklyn Heights for kicks. I can't imagine Em being that twisted—not the Em I know. I check over my shoulder to see if anyone's following me. No one. I feel faint but make it back to the apartment, where I lie on my side on the bed staring at the phone. I want the Talent Killer bad.

The phone rings—the landline.

I get up and answer with, "Dawn?"

"Matt."

"Yes."

"Who's Dawn?"

"This isn't Dawn?"

"You don't recognize my voice?"

"Who is this?"

"*Lauren.* Remember me?"

"Lauren, how'd you get this number?"

Whoever's calling—after reading about that hunter playing that clown game, I can't trust that this is her—pauses to sip something audibly.

"From your lady-friend Em," she says.

"She gave you this number?"

"Yes. We had a nice chat when you two were here the other night. She likes you, Matt. A lot. She reminds me of myself when I first met you."

"She's in for some serious disappointments then."

Lauren says nothing. No laugh, no chuckle, nothing.

Why is she calling? I think.

No.

No way is she the killer.

"So here we are," I say for lack of anything better.

"Yes. Here we are. Though Blaine thinks I'm calling you only to send along our condolences."

"Your condolences and his?"

"Yes."

"Well, thank you for that."

"How are you taking it?"

"Other than wanting to kill someone, I'm fine."

"Oh, Matt."

"What."

"You still can be really funny."

I say nothing.

Then I say, "Anyway, thanks for asking. Listen, I'm not exactly feeling on top of the world, so—"

"Just let me say something, Matt. Just give me another second. I'm really sorry, Matt. Not only about Hendee, but also about…you know, everything."

"I appreciate you saying that."

"But I'm not only saying it. I'm feeling it. And I've been feeling it for a very long time."

It occurs to me that, despite my sadness about Hendee, I'm happy to know this. Does this mean I still love this woman? I wonder. Maybe I simply need anyone right now, I think, but I realize that I do also like hearing the sound of her voice.

"Matt?" I hear.

"Yes."

"You don't have anything to say about whether you can forgive me? Or at least about whether you can accept my apology?"

"To be honest, I have plenty to say. It's just that I'm—you know, kind of overwhelmed right now."

"By what I just said?"

"That and what happened to Hendee."

"No doubt. And again, I'm so sorry about his passing. If you need anything at all, anything, even just a shoulder to cry on, you can text me. I keep my phone on all night, and once Blaine passes out, he's dead to the world."

My smartphone pings. I check it and see it's an email from Dawn.

"Sounds good," I say to Lauren. "But right now I need to go."

"You're still pissed off at me."

"No. I'm not. Truly. I just really need to go."

"Can you just *say* you forgive me, Matt?"

"Lauren, you don't want me to have said it just because—"

"Talk more later?"

"Sure."

"Gator?"

"Yes. Gator."

"Maybe lunch? Maybe dinner again? Blaine's not always here, you know."

"We'll figure out something."

"Talk later," she says, and I hang up and tap up Dawn's email: *Got it and reviewing it. You hanging in there?*

I email her back with, *Call me?*

Again, I stare at the smartphone screen, waiting.

This time she calls within moments:

"Hey," I say. "What do you think?"

"I think this Bowers guy—or whoever he is—will be on the list."

"Harnischfeger said so?"

"Not yet, but I forwarded it to him."

He's talking to Jonas, I think, but I'm worried Jonas might be listening in, so I don't say that.

"But in my view," Trinko says, "those sample chapters the guy sent you were fairly disturbing either way."

"What do you mean 'either way'?"

"I mean whoever wrote them is either the Talent Killer or merely some schlock who's been watching the news lately and decided to write a novel based on what's going on. Unfortunately for us, the longer time goes on, the more we need to consider that second possibility also."

"So, okay, should I get back to him? I could ask if he wants to meet me—"

"Not yet."

"Why not? This guy's out there! He could be ready to—"

"Not until Harnischfeger gives you the green light."

"Okay."

"Also, Matt? We need to talk about something else first, if you don't mind."

"Why would I mind?"

"Because it's personal."

"As long as that's okay with Harnischfeger, lay it on me."

"I *think* it's fine with Harnischfeger."

Jonas, I think. She knows more about Jonas's envy of Hendee than she's told Harnischfeger.

But then she says, "It's about that call you just took, Matt."

"What call?"

"On your landline."

"You were listening in?"

"Yes. And you and I both have work to get back to, so I'll make this quick: unofficially speaking—you know, civilian to civilian—I think you should proceed cautiously."

"With Lauren?"

"Yes. With Em as well, though you already know why you need to keep your guard up around Em. But regarding Lauren, I just wanted to say that, from my perspective—I mean, given the way I see things personally, as a, you know, woman—you should probably steer clear."

"But she and I have things to work out. As you probably heard."

"That's what she's leading you to *believe*, Matt. I'm just letting you know I think that woman is trouble. I think she was selfish back when she cheated on you with Blaine, and I think selfishness like that never goes away. I mean, she strikes me as a woman who's so full of herself she can't stop creating drama that ends up making her the prize."

"But—"

"Just let me just finish, Matt. You have to understand this from a woman's perspective. So if you'll just hear me out."

"Go ahead."

"Your ego, my friend, has been *bruised.* Severely. Not shattered beyond repair, obviously—after all, you had it in you to charm Em. But definitely bruised, Matt, by what Lauren did when she first slept with Blaine. *Plus* you need to consider the possibility that the woman you're into now—Em—might want to kill you. Do you hear that, Matt? Have you accepted that possibility emotionally and not just in your mind? Not to mention a good friend of yours was just killed, possibly by this very same woman you're rebounding with. So altogether, Matt, I'd be remiss if I didn't tell you that, despite all your rehab in Sing Sing, that's quite an emotional cocktail you're being asked to throw down the hatch."

I'm nodding. I'm lost for words. I'm trembling again.

Dawn adds, "To put it more directly still: you have some serious issues."

Wow, I think, not sure whether to be touched or offended.

"Did you hear that, Matt?" she asks.

"Yes," I'm able to say. "I did."

"And it makes sense to you?"

"It does," I say, much as if Dawn asked me right now, I'd say Lauren loved me all along and simply made a drunken mistake when she first slept with Blaine.

"Though now you're having your doubts, aren't you?" Trinko asks.

"About your theories?"

"Yes."

"To be honest, yes, I am."

"Of course you are, Matt. Because you have an ego, and a male one at that. Which is a good thing in your case; otherwise, for you personally speaking, all would be lost. But even with that in mind, I need to impress this upon you, sir: Stay away from both of those women. In Em's case because she's a suspect, in Lauren's because, as a person in *any* capacity, she will never do you any good."

My face, I realize, is hot. As is my neck and the top of my chest. I'm breathing faster, harder. It feels as if a life's worth of thoughts is rushing through my mind.

Surely I can't focus, and just as surely I'm dumbfounded, maybe by pride, maybe by anger, maybe by something else. I consider admitting all of this to Trinko, right now, pretty much as it's occurring to me, but figure someone else with the Bureau, if not Harnischfeger himself, is listening in, so all I say is, "Got it."

"Does that mean you agree?" she asks.

"Yes."

"So keep away from both of them *at least* until this investigation's over, Matt. Seriously. The investigation alone is enough for you to negotiate."

"You're right," I say, and I picture that tough, been-through-it-all, slightly hurt expression that crossed Em's face within moments after our eyes first met.

"Does that mean you will?"

"Will what?"

"Keep away from them."

"Yes. Yes, it does."

"Good," Trinko says. "Hey, I got three new texts here I need to respond to, so I really need to excuse myself."

And then, as abruptly as I got off the phone with Lauren minutes ago, the line goes dead.

21

I receive zero phone calls between the one from Trinko and the morning of Hendee's funeral. During this time, my contact with the outside world—other than when I leave the apartment to hit the bodega—is pretty much all about reading queries. The only contact I have with the Bureau occurs the day before Hendee's funeral, when I receive a businesslike email from Trinko that lets me know Richard Bowers has not made the suspect list, because neither the physical address nor the phone number on his writing sample exists. As Trinko put it: *The person who's behind the email address apparently lives in Bangkok. So, for now at least, this suspect is beyond your purview.*

At 11:30 that night, I receive a query worth forwarding. It purports to be sent by a woman in Paterson, New Jersey, pitches a "family saga" about a wealthy, unmarried woman who lives with her parents who drink heavily, and who herself is arrested for a DUI after she struck a bicyclist and all but killed him. The attached writing sample as well brings Em to mind—I can hear her voice in its sentences, see her smile and tiny, quick fret as I read its dialogue. I don't want to forward it to the Bureau but convince myself I need to. I fall asleep that night thinking about it.

On the morning of Hendee's funeral, Em laces her way through my thoughts. I dread speaking at the funeral with anyone other than her. I have nothing to say to anyone else, I think. As I shower and shave, I think through a few things I could mention about Hendee if asked to eulogize him: his candor, his honor, his wit, his decades of persistence in the face of what most people considered failure. I owe it to him to say these things publicly, I tell myself. Still, I want only to talk with Em.

And when I hear a quiet knock on the apartment door, I

hope it's her. I open the door only to see Jonas, who lunges toward me and grabs my neck. He's choking me, or trying to. Though he hasn't shut the apartment door behind him, suggesting maybe he's doing this in jest? He squeezes my neck harder, causing that first click I heard in Considine's throat, and I'm flailing without contact in my effort to land a punch. I'm scared, the breaths I'm trying to take going nowhere.

Finally, Jonas lets go, and I get oxygen down.

I'm barely able to yell, "What the shit!"

He closes the door behind us, strides past me and across the apartment. Stops at the window overlooking the work being done.

"You ratted me out," he says quietly. He turns and glares at me, his horse face narrower, deep hurt in his eyes.

"I did?" I ask.

"Yes!"

"To whom?"

"To *whom*. To the Harn! Someone told him I write poetry, and the fact is, doofus, you're the only person who knew."

"Not true, man," I say. I cough, swallow hard to rid my throat of a tickle. "People in your office also knew. According to them, you left pieces of your cinquains on your desk."

Jonas raises a finger, stops himself from speaking. He's blushing, I notice.

"It's your own fault, bro," I say.

He frowns, turns, looks out the window. Someone on the roof next door begins jackhammering.

"I asked you never to tell anyone," he says.

"And I didn't. But then Hendee was killed. Put yourself in my shoes, man. Seriously. You would've lied for someone who might have killed your best friend?"

"Well, I didn't kill Hendee."

"How do I know?"

He removes a new wire and a roll of tape from a back pocket. "Because I'm here."

"How do I know Harnischfeger sent you?"

"Hey, if I wanted to kill you, bro, you'd be lying on the floor right now."

I consider this.

"Whatever," I say.

"No, not whatever. So then you *did* tell Harnischfeger I write poetry?"

"You realize the spot you put me in—trying to protect you while also trying to make sure he didn't send me back to Ossining?"

Jonas shrugs.

"For the record, man, I walked the tightrope. Didn't lie, didn't rat you out explicitly either. Nothing I said to him, if he was recording me, could've been used against you. Not to mention you apparently *want* to be a poet, so if you think about it, I covered for you big-time."

Jonas considers this. He still appears miffed, maybe more at himself than at me, maybe at the Talent Killer for fraying the trust between us.

"Plus look at the bottom line," I say. "I didn't lie to the FBI, you didn't get fired."

"Yeah, but it wasn't fun, man—having that sit-down."

"Still, you survived."

"That's one way of looking at it, I guess," he says, and he reaches behind his back for what proves to be a matte black handgun, which he aims at my face, steadying it with both hands.

"Bro, bro, bro," I say.

He smiles, aims the gun at the floor, holds it out toward me.

"Anyway, now you got yourself something that shows the Harn likes you," he says.

"What?"

"Take it, man. It's your service weapon."

"Isn't a little training supposed to be involved?" I ask, and I take the gun.

"Safety," he says, pointing. He clicks it off, clicks it on. "There's your training."

"Uh-huh."

"Go ahead and click it off. So you're sure you know how. Just in case."

I turn off the safety, point the gun at the cheap light fixture overhead. "One quick round of target practice?" I ask kiddingly.

"No, and not funny," he says. "Just so you know, Trinko's putting the chances of the Talent Killer being at the funeral parlor as extremely high."

"Like what percentage high?"

"Like in the nineties."

I put the safety back on, slip the gun nose-first between me and the front of my waistband, right side.

"I recommend you holster it in the rear," he says. "For obvious reasons."

"Got it," I say, and I do that.

He gestures for me to unbutton my shirt, which I do also.

"Did she say ninety-what?" I ask.

He's patting one end of a piece of tape against my chest when he says, "She put it at ninety-eight."

"You think it's Em, don't you," I say.

"I don't know what to think."

We say nothing while he finishes taping.

"Do *you* think it could be Em?" he asks.

"No."

"That's not good, Matt."

"Just being honest."

"Everyone's a suspect now, Matt. Everyone. And remember, you're now armed and able to take out pretty much anyone, so your role in this investigation just got a lot more serious."

"What do you mean, 'pretty much'?"

"Well, there's always the suspect who draws and fires before you can."

"And you think that suspect could be Em."

Jonas eyes me as if to come clean and say, *Not really.*

But he says, "Yes."

Then we do a soundcheck, and I realize that being armed

sort of calms me. It's not that I'm not keyed up, because I am keyed up. It's just that I feel a sense of admirable purpose, something I rarely felt when I was hawking manuscripts.

And I feel this way as Jonas and I leave the apartment and cab to the old-school funeral parlor in Chinatown. Inside the room where Hendee's casket waits, I notice Jenn, the young writer Jonas and I met while posing undercover in Nate's Coffee in Brooklyn. Em, to my dismay, is not here. But Hendee's sister Marnie is—I know this because Jonas nods in her direction and whispers, "His sister the nun."

She's standing all alone toward the front. I feel bad for her, head toward her.

"I'm Matt," I say. "Connell. I was his literary agent."

"Matt Connell, how good of you to come. He was always beyond grateful for everything you did."

I count this as bullshit but let that thought go. She reaches out with both arms, as if for a hug. I oblige, keeping my distance so there'll be no way she'll feel the gun.

"I'm sorry," I say.

She nods, holds on. "Thanks," she says. She lets go and stands on her toes and kisses my cheek, a nun's kiss, nothing special. Not a suspect, I think, but Jonas, standing behind me, says, "We should probably sit." He takes my elbow, leads me toward the very back row of chairs. He sits in the corner on the left, gesturing for me to sit directly to his right, which I do. At the sight of the casket ahead, my throat catches.

Then Lauren walks in. Leading Blaine, she heads up the aisle and sits about six rows in front of us. I have to admit she's rekindling something in me. She faces straight ahead, letting Blaine take the seat beside her. She's apparently determined not to turn to face me.

Then Em walks in.

Damn, I think, because the sight of her fills me with joy.

Okay, I think.

Collect yourself.

Other people are entering, taking seats, some of them

checking me out. A few exchange subdued nods. Jonas's phone is out and on his palm. He's looking up between glances at texts. Only now do I notice he hasn't shaven.

At some point, a priest walks in. Roughly as short as Hendee was, he ambles over to the podium. Father Ed, he calls himself, and he gives a sermon about how he's never known a poet but also wonders if anyone ever really knows a poet. He claims to have met Hendee at a monthly martini hour held in a church in Chinatown to get people interested in religion. My guess is he's thought through at length the insights he's imparting on us—about the certainty of life after death, about the power of love. He seems sure that he's smarter than all of us. He's not the Talent Killer, I think, but the longer he speaks, the more he seems intent on proving he's a nice guy, and the more I wonder if he'll end up on the list.

Then Doreen goes up, from the very back of the room— apparently she walked in late. Jonas is watching her closely. She chokes up as she talks about how fulfilled Hendee made her feel even though she'd known him for such a short period of time. I believe she's innocent, but Jonas's opinion is of course what will matter to Harnischfeger most. She stops talking to unfold a piece of paper, taking a while. By the time she appears ready to read, the paper's rattling loud enough to hear through the mic. It's a poem she took from the desk in Hendee's tiny place on Mott the night they met, she admits. Hendee said it was among the poems of his that were always rejected, she explains. He told her he believed no one wanted to publish it because the publishing world preferred to view him as being a bad person. She admits she stole it from him because she thought they'd never see each other again. She holds up her hand, then makes it clear they did see each other again, that he was the gentlest, most thoughtful man she'd ever dated.

Then she's speaking quietly about Hendee's willingness to let her be herself. She's trembling. It's painful to watch. She says she needs to stop talking, but that what she really needs to do, for his sake and ours, is read the poem, which is titled "July."

She holds it up again for everyone present to see it. She gathers
herself best she can, then reads:

> his better days behind him
>
> the man sat
> in a rowboat past dusk
>
> calm despite the ripples
>
> the trees on the hill
> as full as he'd imagined them
> in February
>
> the lake seemingly his
>
> July would end soon
> & the people in the houses
> where more trees once stood
>
> would force themselves
> out
> for their year's only boat ride
>
> they missed this night
> he thought
>
> the one good one
>
> still now he rowed
> into the bay
>
> toward the dock
>
> on which 3 raccoons
> cracked shells

of snails he couldn't see

eat away
he thought

have the strawberries
too

the raspberries

the largest raccoon
noticed him

her paws at her snout

another shell cracked

& another

I can sit here all night
the man thought

I am better

here

than anywhere

Her voice barely manages to convey that last word. She
clutches the podium. Em rushes up, hugs her, holds her. Says
something in her ear so softly the mic can't pick it up.

And as she helps Doreen return to the back of the room,
I can't stop myself from standing and walking toward both of
them. Em is asking her if she's sure she's okay, and Doreen
nods, and Em is almost as soon facing me, her irreplaceably
gorgeous face pinning mine, stopping me cold. She could be

the killer, those bright black eyes tell me, but they also assure me she'll be the woman I'll die having loved most.

And as she steps into the aisle, we hug. Probably we're startling everyone, but I don't care. It's a hug that goes on awhile, most of it awkward, in some regards almost ferocious—we are gripping and regripping each other as if trying clumsily to finish something we've barely begun. As if admitting to the world, even to the Bureau itself, that if ever we're near each other again, we will lack control.

22

Jonas remains somber as we leave the funeral parlor and make our way past the cameras and reporters and into a cab. He says nothing but "214 Duane" to the cabbie, then faces his phone. He's not texting or calling. He's scrolling. He stays quiet for so long he must be thinking about a violent death of his own.

"You okay, bro?" I ask.

He shrugs.

Then he says, "I didn't like what happened in there."

"What do you mean?"

"When you hugged her. Why'd you have to *hug* her, man? She's a suspect for Chrissake."

"Because—because that's what people do at funerals with people they like."

"Not when they work for the Bureau, they don't."

"So I hugged her, Jonas? What's the big deal?"

"It's the way she did it, with her hands all over you. But mostly, the look on her face. Her left hand was down near the back of your waistband, and all of a sudden—and for just a tiny moment—she looked very, very scared."

"You saying you think she felt the gun?"

"You tell me. Did she?"

I try to remember the hug best I can. What comes to mind is how spontaneous it seemed, how some kind of soap or perfume had her smelling like lavender, how my mind sprinted off into thoughts about a future with her, bright thoughts about me and her getting together as soon as the Talent Killer's behind bars.

"No," I say. "At least I don't think she did."

"So it's possible she did."

"I didn't say that."

"Well, man, we don't have time to jack around here: did she feel it or not?"

"I'm telling you flat-out honestly. I don't know."

"Then she felt it, Matt. You're working undercover for the Bureau, bro—you're no longer just having lunches with people and sending them flowers—or whatever the hell you did as a literary agent—so for safety's sake, your safety and mine, let alone everyone in this city, we'll damn well assume she felt it."

Who cares if she felt it? I want to say. *She loves me!*

But I don't say this. Instead I merely say, "Fine. She felt it."

"Which means we need to report this to Harnischfeger."

"We do?"

He nods. "You want to, or you want me to?"

I can't bear the thought of Harnischfeger knowing I failed to follow his do-not-touch orders. I'm miffed because I never asked for the gun in the first place.

"Let me tell him," I say.

"Well, do it soon."

"How soon?"

"As soon as this guy drops you."

"Okay."

But it's not okay, because Jonas goes back to scrolling, and then texting, which he continues to do even after we've rolled to a stop and I've gotten out of the cab.

"Later," I say, peering in as I'm about to shut the door, but he doesn't so much as glance.

Inside the apartment, I feel a tightness in my chest. I tell myself it's because of the gun, but as I watch the men on the roof next door do their work, I know it's because of what Em and I meant by the hug.

I take out my phone wanting to call her. I consider calling Lauren instead—I need to be able to talk with someone who knows me, the real me, but of course calling Lauren would only complicate things. I draw a glass of water from the bathroom sink and drink most of it but feel emptier. I check my phone. Nothing but emails, all of them queries at that. I compose a text to Harnischfeger in which I admit to him that "it's possible that suspect Em Fontaine felt my service weapon during the embrace she and I shared just after Doreen Archer's eulogy." I reread those words twice, knowing that they jeopardize my ties with the Bureau—as well as acknowledge that some part of me, the rational part, has admitted that, yes, Em might well be intent on bringing about my death.

I hit send.

The rest of the day collapses in on me. My mind ricochets between wishing Em would text and wondering if she's fantasizing about dismembering me. I don't want to leave the building, because if I do I should probably take the gun, and I don't want to touch the gun. Killing Considine was enough, I keep telling myself.

I grow lonely, worse than I felt in Sing Sing. To cope I read queries, which are now flooding in. Clearly there's been coverage of Hendee's funeral on the local news, because a good eighty percent of the queries are from Manhattan, Queens, Brooklyn, or the Bronx.

After the men on the roof of the building next door have quit their jackhammering and gone home, I realize that, despite my continued lack of hunger for food, I should probably eat. I venture out for another bodega-made chicken with pesto sandwich. The counter worker says nothing but, "Swipe?"

The rest of the evening and most of the night pass with me wide awake. The only time I doze, Em appears in a dream in which she's a painted turtle, the two blood-red stripes on her neck making her more irresistible. A married woman in the dream, not Lauren but some woman who looks like Lauren, keeps telling me to throw Em into a lagoon, but I keep holding on to Em, even as she hisses at everyone, including me.

Three p.m. passes the next day without word from her, Jonas, Trinko, or Harnischfeger. It occurs to me that, chances are, the Bureau has moved beyond me completely. Maybe I'm not officially gone, I tell myself, but when it comes to helping with this investigation, I'm clearly on the bench. I muster the courage to call Jonas, reach only voicemail, leave a message he doesn't return, call and leave another message to no avail. Same with the texts and emails I send him. I assume these moves of mine are being monitored by someone at the Bureau if not Jonas himself. In my mind, this means I'm toast.

The only emails I receive other than queries are ads for online dating. The queries are from writers whose talent pales compared with Hendee's, and they lack Em's charm as well as the professionalism of Jonas, Trinko, and Harnischfeger. And none convey enough violence for me to forward. Most are lacking severely in plot, casting doubt on my future as a literary agent too.

That night and the next drag on with me on the Bureau's bed reading one bland query after another. Waiting for an email or text to come in from someone I know personally. Receiving nothing of the sort.

It's in the middle of the third night after Hendee's funeral that I decide to contact Em. My reasoning is that if I can't work for the Bureau, I should at least try to salvage any connection remaining between me and the only person I'm crazy about. But because calling or texting or emailing her would assure my official release from the Bureau, I'll write her a letter and mail it via an old-school USPS mailbox—and to be extra careful, I'll mail it before dawn. To keep the GPS in my FBI-issued phone from tracking me, I'll leave the phone in the apartment when I head out to find a painted-blue box. I'll keep my face down, avoiding high-tech surveillance best a guy in Manhattan can.

My letter to Em is one I scrawl on the back of Hendee's poem "Hope," which is still in the back pocket of the khakis I was wearing when he gave it to me. The upshot of this letter is I want to meet her at four in the morning three nights from now, at "that really old diner with the high tin ceiling." I also ask her not to contact me in the meantime, by any means whatsoever. I do not mention why, because, I assure myself as I write, I'd rather she not suspect I'm losing my mind.

I wait to leave the apartment that night until Chelsea's as

dark as it gets. I walk to what I now consider my bodega, hoping it's twenty-four-hour, which it is, and that it sells stamps, which it doesn't. The cashier sells me a used envelope for a dollar and lets me use his own Scotch tape for free. He himself does not have stamps. The fifth patron to arrive does. This patron is easily eighty-five years old, and wants a twenty for her "only emergency stamp." She mutters angrily about how she'll need to visit a post office branch the next day, how rude to her postal workers always are. In exchange for the stamp, I use the Bureau's debit card to buy her thirty dollars' worth of bottled water and white cheese rice cakes.

Then, with no traffic approaching, I wander until I see a blue box and mail the letter.

Doubtless I've again chosen Em over the Bureau.

Then again, I might soon share a meal with the only remaining source of joy in my life.

What choice, really, did I have?

23

The restlessness I endure while waiting for the next three days to pass is worth mentioning only briefly. You have an imagination. Then comes the night after those three days. Please, I think again and again as 4:00 a.m. approaches. Please be there.

I brush my teeth and tongue twice, switch my phone to airplane mode, trusting that, as long as I'm offline, chances are zilch that the Bureau will know what I'm up to. I also hide my service weapon between the mattress and box spring. It's 3:39 when I depart.

To avoid attention en route, I resist the temptation to jaywalk. I want to be with Em but don't want to be noticed—it's that simple. I enter the old diner, see only four seated patrons, none of them her. I picture her in the arms of some other man, someone powerful and better-looking than I.

No, I think.

As strong as it feels for you, she must feel it too.

Maybe she's just playing it cool.

I point to the booth she and I sat in when she and I were here, ask the cashier near the entrance if I can take it. She nods yes. I sit exactly where I sat then, pretend to read my phone so I won't appear as eager as I feel.

4:00 a.m. passes without her.

4:10.

4:20.

Then, at 4:24, the tall glass door opens and in she flows, stopping the moment she sees me.

Jesus Christ, I think—she looks that good.

And she's smiling at me. As she walks over, I wonder: Is this real?

She sits opposite me. She extends a hand and I take it. Smoothly enough, I kiss the back of it. We hesitate a little but then proceed like any other night. She's searching my face for something. If it's commitment, fine. If I had a billion women to choose from, she'd be the one.

She says, apparently shyly, "That's a great poem you sent."

"What poem?"

"On the back of your note."

"Oh. Right. That was Hendee's."

Her eyes, black as ever, shift the tiniest bit to her right, toward the darkness on the other side of the window.

No way could she have killed Hendee, I think.

No way did she kill anyone.

"Can I ask why we needed to meet at this particular hour?" she asks.

"Because. There are some…exigencies you should probably be aware of."

"Well? You wanna lay 'em on me? Or should we first get the French toast going on the griddle?" She pulls the paper napkin out from beneath her silverware, unfolds it, tucks it into the collar of her white silk blouse.

"Hate to say it, but I think we should talk first."

"And eat later?" she says with a smirk.

I nod. I'd like to smirk back but can't.

"The first thing," I say, and my throat catches.

She notices this.

Asks, "What is it?"

I say all the words quickly, as if they're one: "The first thing is that I love you."

She freezes, mouth open so wide I can see some of her tongue. Her hand's still on the white napkin over her chest, her bob striking me as even more fashionably tousled than it was when we first met, all of her as motionless as death.

She says, "Is that right?"

"Yes. It is."

She looks at me as if she could never fear anyone. "What

I'm saying, buster, is that I thought we established that already."

"We did?"

She nods. "At Hendee's funeral? Not to bring him up again—and not to make light of matters of the heart—but, wow, you sure did come off as a sap with that hug."

I'm not in a mood to joke around. Nor do I want to argue.

"And you didn't?" I ask.

She blushes then. It's the first time I've seen her blush, and all it does is make me want her more.

"I guess I did," she says. "Now can we have our carbs?"

"Okay, but there's one more thing before a waiter shows up. Another big thing. Which may or may not be a secret."

"Ooh, a secret."

"This is kind of serious, Em."

She fights off a grin by pressing her lips together. Her eyes stay lit. I don't want to tell her, much as I feel I owe it to her. It would be so much easier to merely eat some French toast and cab to one of our places and disrobe.

"I think you should maybe leave the country," I say. "At least for a while."

She goes stone-faced.

Pale.

She says, "What?"

"You're being investigated for something. And you very might well be arrested soon. So if you want to avoid all the questioning and lawyering up and possibly some time behind bars, you should probably—maybe even tonight, if you have access to a private jet—fly to…I don't know…someplace with a kickass beach that happens to not give a shit when it comes to extradition? I mean, my sense is you have the money."

Again, her mouth is open. I want to cover it with mine.

"Matt, why would you say something like that?"

"Because I know stuff."

"But how? How would you know about anything whatsoever along those lines?"

"Because I've learned a few things."

"But...what? I mean, what about me that would cause you to...talk to anyone about anything like that?"

Tell her you're with the Bureau, I think, and they will find out—somehow—and send you back to Sing Sing.

But I do love her—that's for damned sure—so what I say is, "For one thing, I know you've been arrested twice for assault."

Her arms fly out sideways, her fingers outstretched. "You're...you're *trolling* me?"

"I wasn't trolling."

"Yes, you were! You were definitely trolling!"

"Fine. I was trolling. And I have every reason to believe you're under investigation for something else—right now, as we speak."

"What in hell am I doing here?" she says, and she yanks the napkin out of her blouse and throws it against the tabletop. With a passion in her eyes I've never seen, she asks, "How can you even...*say* that?"

"That's not the question, Em. The question is, what are you going to do now that I've gone out on a limb to tell you? I mean, are you going to leave the country or not?"

Disbelief is flooding her eyes.

Then some sort of realization.

She *does* want to leave? I think. She wants to take me with? She's blinking fast, maybe choosing her words, maybe, I hope, figuring out precisely how to ask.

Finally, and very quietly, she says, "You think I'm the Talent Killer."

"Absolutely not! I think I've told you some crucial truths about what might happen to you, and I think I was doing you— and maybe us—a huge favor."

And in my mind I've said this in a tone that assures her I'm on her side and then some, but she slides out of the booth, snatches her napkin back off the table, throws it at me, and marches off.

"Em, what else was I supposed to say?" I shout as the napkin floats down.

Two older patrons are glaring at us, then at me as she yanks open the glass door.

Then all of us are watching her stride out.

I sit still as the door closes, hopeless about her return. I don't move until I imagine I'm no longer the center of attention, at which point I sip from my water. I notice a young man, obviously not born into wealth, watching me from two tables away. He catches my eye and shrugs as if to say, *What can you do?* I nod, sip more water. Look down at my phone. Read a query I received earlier in the day. It's for a memoir written by a happily married eighty-eight-year-old grandmother of twelve named Mabel T. Harrington, and its first five pages aren't bad. But what good, I wonder, have all the books in the world done?

A waiter arrives and I ask him for a beef noodle soup and a carton of milk to go, and the check immediately if possible. He nods, heads off, returns promptly and hands me all three, and I pay the cashier with the Bureau's card, adding a twenty-dollar tip. The soup and the milk go to the first homeless person I see, a disheveled, cross-legged woman doubtless in need of more than just food. She thanks me and says, "God bless you," and I continue to my building without looking at my phone. As soon as I'm in the apartment with the door locked, I turn off all the lights and pull the blue drapes until they overlap, then lie on the bed with a forearm across my eyes. But I soon know I'm incapable of sleep. All I can do is think about my twenty-eight minutes. And then all I can think about is Em.

Then I hear keys clinking behind the apartment door, and the door opens, and in walks Trinko, appearing taller and thinner than she did last I saw her, clutching the strap of a small black canvas bag slung over her shoulder.

"Where've you been, Matt?" she asks.

Clearly she knows where. Clearly she's trying to catch me in a lie, thus giving her cause to terminate me on the spot.

I get out of bed and say, "Maybe, Detective, you should tell me."

"You've been with Em."

"So you know."

"Of course I know, Matt. I work for the Bureau."

"But how? I switched the phone to airplane mode."

She shrugs. "Didn't matter. It was your shoes. There's a tracking device in each."

"Since I left Sing Sing?"

She nods, gives me a cynical wink. "I can watch you—a little green dot—walk down any street on Google Maps. If I zoom in on my screen, the green dot becomes two little feet walking down a given block. I can tell if you're standing still or jogging or running or jumping. If you're jumping, I can learn how high to within one-one-hundredth of an inch."

"And the Bureau really thinks such detail is necessary?"

She shrugs. "Plus we've had a device on Em herself for a while."

"Seriously?"

"The Bureau emails her a forty percent-off coupon for cam-isoles from an email address that appears to be from Blooming-dale's. She clicks up the coupon on her phone and, boom, whether or not she buys, we have her walking around with a tracking device as long as she has her phone on her person. Which of course she does, because everyone does."

"So you've been tracking Em for *how* long?"

"About, I don't know, a week? If her phone moves more than fifty consecutive feet in one direction, my phone takes special notice—and at night I set my phone to also buzz loud enough to wake me when this happens, so then it can show me, on my screen, which of our suspects is going where. In the case of your little rendezvous just now, I saw that Em had left her residence, and that she was walking to the same diner you were walking to. It's not rocket science, Matt. Putin's thugs have been bugging Americans' phones this way since 2014. Anyway, I need you to turn in your service weapon."

"You do?"

For a moment I treasure, she merely studies me up and

down, as if maybe she has the discretion to keep me in the Bureau's employ and out of Sing Sing.

But then she says, "It's over, Matt. You were instructed to stay away from that woman, and you screwed up. Twice."

Heat rushes up my throat, into my ears. I raise the mattress, gesture for her to go ahead and take the gun, which she does.

She checks its safety to make sure it's on, slips it into the canvas bag, offers her hand, and we shake and exchange goodbyes.

But after she leaves, I follow her down the hall and out of the building. She's already begun west on the treeless sidewalk on Duane when I shout, "Can I offer the Bureau one last opinion?"

She stops, turns, shrugs. Gives me one last nod.

I take a few steps closer. "For the record," I call, "I think Em Fontaine is innocent."

"We know you do, Matty."

"I'm serious, Trinko. She's innocent! I know this like no one else could!"

"You're in love, Matty," she says somewhat respectfully as she turns back around. Then, over her shoulder, she calls, "We wish you luck."

And with that she continues on, into one of those rare unmitigated silences in Manhattan, the kind that can envelop an entire block just before the sun comes up.

24

Days go by without word from the Bureau. Or, for that matter, from Em. I pass time by reading emailed queries that don't interest me in any regard. I speculate that since there's been no televised news about an arrest, Em has either been removed from the Bureau's list or heard me loud and clear and left the country.

My smartphone and Bureau-issued debit card continue to work, though, suggesting the Bureau will make good on its promise to provide me room and board till the end of the month, but the end of the month is coming fast.

In fact, I think late one morning, today is the summer solstice.

Time to *live*, I think.

To move on, to find a place of your own.

Buoyed by these thoughts, I stroll from Duane to the branch of the bank I used before my twenty-eight minutes, the bells-and-whistles one on Fifty-Sixth and Broadway, where I knew most everyone and most everyone knew me.

It'll be good to see Ron, I tell myself en route.

But Ron is no longer working at the branch on Fifty-Sixth. In fact, a sign in the window informs me the branch on Fifty-Sixth has moved to Sixty-Third.

And my visit to the branch on Sixty-Third is indeed one in which, for the first time, in the real, everyday world, I experience the full brunt of the stigma. The sudden stillness of the person when they see your account's been inactive for years, and that your last listed known address includes a prisoner number in Sing Sing. The moment or two (or three or four) of discomfort as they gather their composure and ability to continue speaking to you. The time burned as they double-check with superiors, supposedly to make sure you are who you say you are—but really, you fear, to make sure their superiors still want to do business with you regarding the savings you put away before your arrest.

I do, however, emerge from that branch with three thousand in cash, a book of ten temporary checks, and a temporary debit card of my own. I've also received assurance from a thirty-some-year-old "vice president" that I can use him as a reference if Scardina's name won't prove reference enough.

In any case, I am up against the possibility of homelessness in Manhattan when my FBI phone rings.

DAVIS, the screen says.

No, I think. Not Blaine. Not now.

"Yes," I say.

"Matt!"

"Blaine?"

"Of course! How are you! Faring well, I take it, since you aren't answering my email?"

"What email?"

"The one I sent last night."

"Must have gotten lost in the barrage. How'd you get this number, by the way?"

"Lauren."

"I see."

"She said you wouldn't mind. Do you mind?"

I can't help but remember Lauren's bare foot pressing the inside of my thigh as Blaine and Em flirted. There's no quick answer about who I should trust—but in that respect, I realize, my life is returning to how it was before my time in Sing Sing, where I couldn't trust anyone. Things were simpler there, I think. Not easier, but simpler.

"Matt?" Blaine is asking.

"Yes?"

"I was asking if you mind."

"Mind what?"

"Me having your number."

"No," I say. "I mean, it's cool." I'm back to being an agent again, I realize. Goodbye integrity. Goodbye fidelity and bravery too?

"So as I mentioned in that email," he says, "if you're willing to give your all toward doing the rewrite, I'm willing to go as high as a hundred thousand up front. Cash."

"Two," I say, even though I'm unsure I want to rewrite as much as a sentence for anyone ever again. What I want is Em. To be wherever she is, to hear her voice, to feel it brighten me if her black eyes can't.

"One twenty-five and that's that," Blaine says, but I hear it in his voice: amicability.

Or is it desperation?

Either way you have him, I think.

"One seventy-five and I'll be there this evening," I say. "But only if your man Marty lands me a decent place to rent first."

"Marty lands you a place in Long Island City and one-fifty," he says.

"In Manhattan and one-seventy-five, brother— you want me to drop everything here to work with you tonight, that's how it's gotta be."

"Hang on," Blaine says, as if he has something more important pressing.

But I know this trick, so I hang up.

And within the count of three, my phone rings.

"This is Matt Connell," I say, as if to a stranger.

"Did you *hang up*?"

"I don't know, man. This phone can be weird. Did I?"

"Fine. Okay. One-seventy-five and Marty finds you a sweet apartment in Manhattan. Be at my place at four-thirty this afternoon."

I hold the phone away from me, let him hear the sounds of the traffic clamoring by. I return the phone to the side of my head and clear my throat.

Then, resolutely, I say, "Sure."

25

Blaine doesn't open the door. Lauren does. And she and I share a loaded moment of searching each other's faces. "You're back," she says.

"You gave Blaine my number."

"I wanted to see you without needing to lie about where we were, so I figured why not have Blaine invite you."

"He's struggling that much with the revision?"

"God, yes."

She motions me toward her and we hug. "So...where is he?" I ask, even though I like inhaling the scent of her hair, feeling how well our bodies still fit together.

"In his office," she says, hanging on. "You know where that is, right?"

"No."

"It's in one of his old properties a few blocks east of here. A redbrick warehouse not far from Steinway—I can show you."

She lets go only to grab my wrist. Pulls me further inside, toward the living room, stops us at the largest of the three couches, kicks off her white satin slippers, sits, curls her legs up under her, pats the cushion beside her.

"This doesn't look like a warehouse," I say.

"Come on. Just one more time of being nice to each other."

It would feel especially good right now. It would happen in that effortless yet feverish way we had, and it would feel damned, damned good.

"Just a few minutes," she says.

"I think maybe we should both quit while we're ahead."

She looks off toward the balcony's view of Manhattan, sighs.

"It's Em, isn't it?" she asks.

"What do you mean?"

"I *knew* it. I knew it by how hard you tried to look like you didn't care when she was flirting with Blaine. And by the way she talked about you before I told her how I messed things up for us. I *knew* it."

I shrug. "What do you want me to say? Em's a very cool person. Do you want me to lie to you?"

She shakes her head no. Stands and walks off and stops to look out the sliding glass doors to the balcony. More than the top third of the Manhattan skyline is obscured by fog, which means Em's window is now facing nothing but gauzy white.

"I just want you to remember I never lied to you either," she says.

"Ever?"

"Ever. I did a stupid thing, Matt, getting caught up with Blaine. I was young, and success like his comes off as sexy when you're young. But I never stopped loving you, Matt. I never stopped loving you, and I always told you the truth—including when you asked if I slept with Considine."

She looks over at me expectantly.

"I need to go," I say. "I told him I was coming here to help him do his rewrite."

Her decision now to face Manhattan rather than me comes as a disappointment. I don't understand exactly why I still care.

"It's not difficult," she says. "Just take a right past the circular driveway and go three blocks, then take a left and go five more. It's about six or seven stories tall, and there's flaking white paint on the side you'll see as you approach. If you look closely at what's left of the paint, you can still make out the name—National something or other."

She heads toward me, passes me en route to the foyer. Sets her hand on the doorknob. Sighs, opens the door, looks out at the elevator bank.

"Go," she says. "Go help your good pal write his goddamned book."

I kiss her forehead kindly and walk out. Wait for the elevator with my back to her. If she's closed the door I haven't heard her do so, and I don't turn around to see. Because I'm a coward when it comes to things like that.

Outdoors, I follow her directions and soon see the faint words National Cold Storage on the painted redbrick wall. I ring the newest doorbell beside the entrance.

Blaine answers the door and says, "Hey, Matt."

He does not seem curious about my having just seen Lauren. He seems intent on work.

"Not to be crass," I say, "but you do have the cash, right?"

"I do. Come on in. I'll get it and make us a drink."

He leads me up concrete stairs flanked by cylindrical steel banisters that appear to have recently been repainted green. On the second-last flight of stairs, we leave the stairwell for an office that takes up the entire floor: antique rolltop desk, four ceiling fans, art deco furniture, king-size bed, mammoth paintings he's sunk a few hundred thousand into easily. The leaded windows overlook various abandoned buildings, parking lots, and the less-impressive eastern view of Queens, but his workspace suggests a superiority of sorts—it's higher than most every building between us and the Atlantic.

He gestures for me to sit. I choose a hardbacked chair. "So this is where it all happens," I say.

He nods. "Scotch? Bourbon? Vodka?"

"Coffee."

"I assume caffeinated?"

"Yes."

He returns to the stairwell and, given the sound of his footfalls, heads upstairs. I notice a rubber-banded manuscript to the left of the laptop on his desk. I tell myself to ignore it until I have the $175K in hand, but the literary agent in me has me curious.

The rubber band snaps as I remove it. The title is *Blizzards*, which I'm guessing he's used because he saw *Fargo*. I flip to a page about three-quarters through to see if he's mustered any suspense—the reason I needed to rewrite *Night of the Solstice* was

he'd drafted 300 pages of "high-minded" thoughts and no story.
He's still playing with uncommon fonts, I notice.

I do my best to read with an open mind:

> She did have smarts, he reminded himself. She set
> her wine glass on the floor beside his desk, stepped be-
> tween him and the window, kept her back to him while
> observing what they could see this many stories up. She
> was dancing a little, swaying, letting her ass brush up
> against him.

Change the word *ass*, I think.

Upstairs, a coffee grinder whines but stops immediately.

"Dammit!" he shouts.

"Take your time!" I shout back.

> She kept dancing, pressing against him. She was try-
> ing to prove to someone, maybe him, that she was sexy
> as well as talented. The talented ones were always like
> that—competitive.

The *talented* ones, I think.

"Tea okay instead?" he shouts.

"Sure!"

I flip a few pages ahead:

> He stepped back. He wanted to see.
> "We no longer care about talking?" she asked haugh-
> tily.
> Why were the talented ones always so damned haugh-
> ty?
> "We're happy just watching?" she asked, still swaying,
> then swaying and pressing herself against him. He went
> jittery. He was salivating. He remembered having lost
> it with the last one because of her haughtiness, yet he
> couldn't look away from this one now.
> He promised himself he'd remain calm. He promised
> himself he'd only watch.

She kept dancing, raised her arms slowly, set her hands against the windowpane.

"Show me," she said.

"Show you what?" he asked.

"How success feels," she answered.

He hated hearing that word out of the mouth of someone like her—success. He hated the implication that he had the success even though she had the talent.

"Be a man and show me," she said, but it was she who was showing him, her fingertips taking hold of the hem of her skirt, raising it amply but not enough for him to see everything.

He stepped toward her, touching only her hair, grabbing hold of more and more of it, creating a ponytail.

No, he thought, but then he thought, Just one.

"Is that showing me?" she said haughtily, and he felt it, and he tried to stop it, and he was sure he could this time, but then he was doing it, pulling the hair gently to see if his hold on it was good, then yanking it, and now, no, it was happening the way it had with the others—she emitted a yelp, but he was yanking again, harder, cruelly harder despite himself, then harder still, and she was screaming, but no one outside could hear with them being this high up. And, yes, yes, it was happening in him, and no, no, he didn't want it to keep happening again, but, yes, he couldn't let go. The thought of the time he'd spent cleaning the blood of the others only angered him more, taunting him, and there was that smart, beautiful head of hers, full of her haughty, talented thoughts, but he had her now, he could show her what happened to haughtiness, he would prove to her what happened to talent when it came to putting together words: It ultimately fell into the wrong hands, and, ultimately, those hands silenced it.

I swipe open my phone, type a text to Jonas quickly as I can:

Am with B. Davis in his warehouse office bldg in LIC and looking @ this in his unpublished ms "the time he'd spent cleaning the blood of the others" and "he would prove what happened to talent when it came to putting together words: It ultimately fell into the wrong hands."

As I hit send I hear, "Couldn't help yourself, huh."

He's there, standing in the doorway to the stairwell, holding two steaming ceramic mugs of tea.

"Guess you caught me red-handed," I say, and I find the icon to call Jonas, tap it, find the icon for speakerphone mode and tap that.

"What part did you read?" he asks.

"About the talented woman dancing for the protagonist. I mean, I assume it was the protagonist."

"Why wouldn't it be?"

"Because in the last sentence I read, he was about to kill her? I mean, I *suppose* that could be a protagonist Sherry would want to publish, but, to be honest, if you want a murderer to be your protagonist, you're asking me to do a heavy lift when it comes to revising this thing."

He walks toward me with the mugs, holds one out.

"Careful," he says. "It's hot."

I take the mug, hold it against my chest. I could fling the tea at him, tackle him, do to him what I did to Considine.

I *want* to fling the tea at him, tackle him, do to him what I did to Considine.

Instead, I say, "Thanks."

"If you think it needs a complete rewrite, Matt, just say so. Now that we're alone here, as far as I'm concerned, what happens between us should be all about honesty."

"You think so."

"I do."

"Then I think it's time for you to fess up about Lauren."

"What?" he says.

"You know what."

"Matt, I married the woman after you were in prison for

almost three years. You told her lawyer you were cool with a divorce, with her moving on to marry me."

"I'm not talking about you marrying her, man."

"Then what are you talking about?"

"Doing what you did when she was married to me."

He feigns surprise and shock, proving he's no better an actor than he is a writer.

Just as unconvincingly he says, "I have no idea what you're talking about."

"So that's it."

"What's what?"

"You're not going to fess up about sleeping with her before that?"

"Matt, she *divorced* you. And I married her. Is that such a crime?"

"So you're trying to tell me you weren't with her before then."

He sips some tea cautiously.

Says, "Yes."

But his eyes go wide, a side of his upper lip twitching.

"So are we good?" he asks. "Can we get into doing the rewrite?"

"Are we still being honest?" I ask.

"Of course."

I glance down at my phone screen, see that my call with Jonas is still intact, trust Jonas has answered it and is listening.

"It strikes me, Blaine," I say, "that there are five unsolved murders out there—I mean, in the real world. Committed by the Talent Killer, I mean. And, well, the pages of yours I just read are about a guy who not only kills as a matter of course, but who also apparently has a thing about his victims having... you know, *talent*."

He sips, or pretends to, staring me down. "So?"

"So if you really want to know why I think Sherry doesn't want to publish this manuscript, I'll tell you: she believes this book is your way of admitting to the world that you, Blaine Davis, are the Talent Killer."

"But obviously," he says, "I'm not the Talent Killer."

"Yet obviously Sherry thinks you are. And she fears that the world will conclude you are if she publishes this book, which would lead to your arrest and, if we go by the pages I just read, your conviction—which from Sherry's point of view would mean goodbye to her cash cow."

"Well, that's just silly thinking on her part, isn't it?"

You are the worst liar, I want to say.

You are going to prison.

"Why is it silly?" I ask.

"Oh, come on, Matt. You don't really believe I could—"

"You keep an office in a *cold storage facility*, man. Meaning there's a huge walk-in freezer in this place, the very kind of thing the Talent Killer is keeping his victims in as he cuts them up before he…distributes them."

"Matty, Matty, Matty. Are you joking with me?"

"Are we still being honest?"

"Of course."

"Then, no, I'm not joking. I'm telling you outright what I think about your manuscript, and what I think about you."

"So that's it. Boom. I'm the Talent Killer."

I nod.

"But how could I own a cold storage facility, and kill writers, and then write a book about a successful guy who kills writers and keeps them in cold storage? How could I possibly be that stupid?"

"It's not that you're so stupid," I say. "It's that you have so much nerve."

"I do?"

"You believe you're so adored by the world you can actually get away with this. Just like you believed, after I wrote and sold *Night of the Solstice* for you, that you could get away with screwing Lauren behind my back."

"But I told you: I didn't sleep with her behind your back. All I did was marry her."

"The problem with that statement being that I know it's a lie."

"And you know it's a lie *how?*"

To mess with his head, I take my time sipping some of my tea. I realize, after I swallow a mouthful, that maybe he put something poisonous in mine.

I glance at it and say, "That's my business."

He offers me a tortured look. "You know what, buddy?" he says. "Let's go. Let's go have you check out the cold storage area downstairs. That way we can end this whole ridiculous line of inquiry. And get down to revising a book which, I'll remind you, is *fiction.*"

"Good," I say.

"Okay," he says, and he nods curtly, reaches into a cubbyhole in the desk, grabs a key ring, and heads off toward the stairwell. I follow, and we begin down.

About halfway down it hits me that he's conned me into heading into the very place he stores his victims, i.e., that if he kills me in there, he won't even need to move me before cutting me up.

But he's dealing with *me*, I think. I check my phone, the screen of which suggests Jonas is still listening—that is, if the transmission works regardless of the thickness of the old concrete walls around me.

At the bottom of the stairs, there's light from a bulb strung up over a narrow corridor. To the right is a wide stainless-steel door with a padlocked handle. He finds the key to the lock and opens the door, and I follow him into an unlit space. Only then does it hit me how easily he found the key.

All four of the walls around us are stainless steel, and the room spans pretty much the entire basement—it's the size of a small parking lot. But it's not cold in the least. In fact, it's uncomfortably warm. He turns off the refrigeration between kills to keep the electric bill down? I think. Regardless, it's darker and warmer still the further in I venture. A cursory glance at the floor and all four walls tells me it's empty.

But the floor, I notice, shines more than the walls.

"See?" he says. "Empty. Are we good?"

"Hang on," I say.

I walk further in.

I'm beyond halfway to the far wall when I first smell it.

Bleach.

Hoping again that the phone can transmit, I shout over my shoulder, "Hate to say it, my friend, but it kind of smells like bleach in here."

"It does not."

I turn around and face him.

Sniff audibly, to see how he'll react.

He folds his arms and says, "Nothing. Right?"

I sniff again.

"Wrong," I say. "That's bleach. I'm definitely smelling bleach."

"Matt, let me just level with you about something, okay?"

"Sure," I say, my face growing warm, my mind eddying with memories of my twenty-eight minutes, my forehead prickling with sweat.

"Between you and me," he says, "you *are* by far the better storyteller. What I'm saying is, I'll admit that your work on *Night of the Solstice* was crucial to my success. But this same talent of yours presents us two problems all these years later. The first is…well, I'll just come right out and say it. No one cares about whether you wrote *Night of the Solstice* twenty years ago—the world cares about what *I* do now. The second is, in situations such as the one you're in presently, thanks to your oh-so-talented imagination, you believe you sense things that don't actually exist."

I shake my head slowly.

Say, "Nice try, loser."

"What does that mean?"

"It means I can still smell what I smell, and I'm telling you, Mr. Bullshit, I'm smelling goddamned bleach."

"Well, I'm telling *you*, Matt, that there's never been a drop of bleach in here."

"Well, I think there has been."

"Why don't you walk a little farther in? Just to make sure. Go ahead, be my guest."

He grabs the door with one hand, as if daring me to risk that, if I head farther inside, he'll lock me in. He does not mention this possibility, though. His dare and my acceptance of that dare are all wrapped up in his glaring at me and my looking off.

Then, to fluster him, I study my phone. For a while I can't find the flashlight app, but when I do, it works splendidly. I'm set to photograph any little smudge. I consider taking a photo of nothing in particular to bluff him into attacking me physically—this would be the nail in his coffin in a court of law. I walk toward the far wall with my back to him, the kind of unspoken dare I learned in Sing Sing: *If you're packing a blade, chickenshit, feel free to bring it. We'll see who's boss here—bring it.*

I stop a foot or so from the far wall, go down to my knees. I crawl, keeping my eyes on the lower half of the wall and the floor. All I need is one tiny splash his mop missed. I see nothing, so I decide to bluff. I stop crawling and stand on my knees, then crouch to face an area of the wall a few inches from the floor, then, more grateful than ever for my smartphone, take a photo.

He says nothing.

Does nothing except stand in that doorway.

Then, near a corner, I see it.

Silver, round, bulbous.

No holes.

A loop underneath for the thread to go through.

And there's thread.

And, holy shit, the thread is eggplant.

That's a kind of purple, Matt, I remember Jonas saying, and I snap a photo of the button.

Then another.

Then a third and a fourth.

I use the hem of my shirt to pick up the button, hold it out toward him, say to him, "Maybe you should tell me whose this is."

"What is it?"

"A button. A woman's button."

"How do you know it's a woman's?"

"There's purple thread in the loop."

He shifts his feet, and a look passes over his face—just for an instant, but I'm sure I saw it: unadulterated fear.

"So?" he says.

"So it's over, Blaine. Thanks to this button, you're going down."

He considers this.

Steps back behind the threshold, closes the door.

Idiot, I think, because I can hear him lock it, which, in the eyes of a jury, will be yet more proof of guilt.

"Blaine," I shout. I step closer to the door. "Don't be stupid. I can set you up with the best criminal lawyers."

"Goodbye, Matt," he says, barely audible through the insulation.

And then he simply lets the silence work on me.

The silence and my growing panic, which causes my face and chest and shoulders to break a sweat.

"Blaine," I yell. "I'm undercover with the FBI. They know I'm here."

I leave it at that, figuring what I don't say from now on will work in my favor.

But again, there's an increase in the heat. I'm not sure if it's from the lack of fresh air, or from me, but it's getting to me, and the darkness around me feels as if it's seeping into me.

"You really think I'm gonna believe that, Matt?" I hear.

I step to within an inch or so of the door so I can speak quietly—I want to sound calm.

I am not calm.

I ask, "Who do you think I was texting upstairs when you walked in on me reading your manuscript?"

Again, I hear nothing.

But now, I think, the truth of everything that's happened between us—today and over the years—has me ahead?

It's merely a matter of letting his mind process it?

"You've got no soul, Blaine," I say, "but you're not an idiot. You knew it was too big of a coincidence that, within days of my release, Hendee was arrested. Hendee's arrest simply made my connection with the Bureau obvious to anyone who thought about it. Which is what you're doing now. You're thinking about it. And you keep coming up with the conclusion that, yes, darn it, your old pal Matt Connell is indeed tight with the FBI."

I hear something stir on the other side of the door.

I might hear other things, some of them said or done by him, but I'm not sure because my mind's spinning with memories of my twenty-eight minutes, of my marriage, of my life, of Em.

Then, through the door, I'm hearing his voice say: "Matt, you're gonna suffocate, okay? With a phone that won't work because you're in Long Island City under tons of concrete and encased in steel."

I check my phone for anything from Jonas—from anyone. Nothing.

I hit the internet icon, get one ellipsis after another.

"Listen, man," I shout. "If I turn out to be gone for even a few hours, the tracking device the Bureau put in this phone will lead them directly here."

I'm not sure the Bureau's tracking devices work through this much concrete, but I've just spoken with a decent amount of bravado.

"That's bad news for you, pal," I shout, "because all I have to do now is send a text telling them you locked me in here as soon as I told you I knew you were the Talent Killer. In which case, if I die in here with this phone, they'll track me and arrest you for killing me—or, if you take the phone out of here to hide it somewhere, my text will transmit and they'll be on you because of *that*."

I wait for him to answer.

For the door to open.

Nothing.

"So there's only one wise option for you, pal," I say. "Buy this button and thread and this phone from me, and buy them before I text the Bureau these photos I just took. And if you open this door immediately—and this offer is for damned sure for a limited time only—you'll get me cheap: half a million each for the button and this thread and the phone, on top of the mill you'll pay me to re-do your book. Two and a half mill total, which is chump change for you, wired from your account to mine, and this button and thread and this phone are yours to destroy, bury, toss in the East River—whatever you want, and then I rewrite your book, and, to make sure we stay best friends forever, I get fifteen percent of everything your books bring in from now on."

I wait.

Breaths become harder to take.

I'm perspiring everywhere.

"We become agent and client again, Blaine—with me being your agent, having a profit motive to keep even your worst secrets. Kind of like we were in the old days, just a little more, you know, sophisticated."

And as I say that word, *sophisticated*, I remove one of my Bureau-issued wingtips. I'll clock him on the head with the heel of it hard as I can, stunning him, probably, given the wrath I feel, knocking him out. Either way, I'll run upstairs and outside to wherever I need to be to get a call through to Jonas.

But after my hands have the shoe high over my head, the door remains shut.

He's still out there, I think.

He's planning his own next move.

"This way my fortune depends on you, buddy," I call through the door. "This way we remain thick as thieves forever."

But I keep holding the shoe well above my head. My shoulders start to tire, then ache. I fear he's gone off to get the weapon he used on the others. I promise myself that, regardless of what he says as he opens the door, I'll not only whap him with the shoe so hard he'll go down, I'll kick the side of his head for good measure.

Not enough to kill him—just enough to assure I survive.

I make these promises to myself repeatedly. I am terrified. I feel capable. There is underlying doubt, too, and there is anger, and, as has always been the case since my twenty-eight minutes, there are memories of Lauren and me when we first married, of Considine and Blaine both out to dinner with me and her when I believed they'd be my clients forever, of the innocence in her voice as she denied having slept with Considine.

Then, all at once, the memories stop, because I'm hearing the clink of keys.

But the door remains motionless.

He's gathering his focus, I think.

Or he's reconsidering your offer?

Or is he realizing what the weapon he's holding could do to him if we struggle and I get hold of it?

Then I see a skinny plane of light: silent as the door has remained, it has opened.

I ready the shoe.

My resolve not to kill, I think, does not mean I won't knock him out.

Then the plane of light thickens, and the door creaks, opening so slowly I wonder if he's gone upstairs and a draft from the corridor is pushing it.

Then I see one of his feet, entering, and I'm putting every bit of the hatred in me into bringing down the shoe, its heel striking the crown of his head.

He is down, lying there, crumpled.

He remains still for so long I'm convinced he's unconscious.

Convinced that, by any measure, I've won, and that the Bureau has won, and that, insofar as it's possible, society has won.

I drop to my knees to make sure he's alive. Warmth wafts again and again out of his nose. I think about how I once considered him a decent friend, how naïve I was back then, how I trusted people in general too easily given how ambitious people in publishing can be. In the back of my mind I know my phone is still switched on—whether it can transmit is, for me now, the only issue.

Certainly not in question is that I'm feeling it again. My Ferrari brain, as Em put it. My embodiment of so many thoughts and emotions at once as to create an uncontrolled sense in me of careening. My fingertips outstretched as I place my hands around a human being's neck.

And, hey, if you're me, you think you can stop this when it happens to you. You think you'll quit doing it in the very next moment, that you're doing it only to humor yourself, but each moment becomes an expression of yourself that needs to be finished, and at some point, you realize you can't stop—and, worse, that you don't want to stop.

And after you've heard that first click in the throat and the man's face begins to turn purple, you know that, now, realistically speaking, there's no way he can kill you. Things inside of his neck and inside of you are breaking, and, if you keep squeezing this hard, hard enough that your own eyes bulge, things in him and you will break beyond repair.

But you keep on.

This, in your hands, is an ugly life, and you, a former friend, are ending it.

26

Time has an odd way of passing after you commit homicide, so how long I sit with Blaine is something I don't know.

But for several minutes at least, I've accepted the possibility that, at any moment, I'll learn through my phone that the Bureau overheard everything, as well as the Bureau's instructions on how I should proceed, officially speaking.

You didn't need to kill him, I think more than once.

You're going back to Sing Sing.

And with those two syllables repeating themselves in my mind—*Sing Sing*—I get up, leave the door open behind me, and walk out and into the narrow, barely lit corridor, then begin climbing the stairs.

On the second-highest stair, I grow dizzy, but I press on.

Then I'm out there, surefooted, standing on the sidewalk where I rang the doorbell, when I believed Blaine's greatest sin was adultery.

It's just after the sunshine on my face starts calming me that the Bureau's vehicles arrive. Three of them, and they all stop across the street. Five plainclothes guys, one of them Jonas, duck out of a sedan painted yellow and black to resemble a cab. The sight of Jonas's horse face underscores my disappointment in myself as his colleague. After all, if I maintain my integrity, there's a heavy truth I will, from now on, always carry with me: I could have allowed Blaine's punishment to be determined by a jury of his peers, but, no, I did not allow that—I determined Blaine's future myself.

And now here I am, toe-to-toe with Jonas.

"You okay?" he asks.

"I'm alive. You on the other end of my call the whole time?"

"Not the whole time. Trinko noticed, from the transmission

from your shoes, that one was like eight feet higher than the other."

"I see."

"She figured either you'd gotten your ass kicked and the dismembering had already begun, or you were about to use one of the shoes to smack the son of a bitch over the head."

"Well, she was right."

"You mean he didn't even land a punch?"

"That's correct."

"And you ended up, what, tying him up? I don't get how you secured him. Did you use your belt? Did you use his?"

"You'll see," I say. "He's still in the cold storage area."

And I leave it at that.

"I take it that's in the basement?" Jonas asks.

I nod, and he heads inside with the rest of them.

I realize that, if I want to try to bolt, now's the time.

And half of me wants to give it a try.

The other half, the half I believe is wise, keeps me standing where I am.

So they send you back? I think.

Three hots and a cot.

As I wait for Jonas to return, I look around. On this particular street, nothing is growing. Not one weed in one crack in one sidewalk. Concrete everywhere. Useless no-parking signs rusted and bent.

For a long time, I stare at a high rise west of me.

I think, Well, shit—at least a few bankers up there are happy.

Then Jonas emerges and heads straight toward me.

"Buddy," he says, eyeing me steadily. "Looks like you went a little overboard."

I shrug.

"That's all you're gonna tell me?" he asks.

I nod.

He studies me closer still. Up, down, sideways. Like he did when he and Scardina and I discussed Hendee's "A Quieter Saturday Night."

"Couldn't help yourself, huh," he says.

I want to say yes but don't. Instead, I exchange with him one of those looks you share with someone you consider your best friend. The kind of look that admits everything the two of you know about each other, all of it, the crazy and the sane both. The kind of look you trust will never be mentioned by either of you to anyone.

"Gotchya," he says.

Which, of course, can mean any of several things.

27

If I believe what Jonas has reported to me by way of his personal phone over the course of the past twenty-four hours, Harnischfeger has plenty of evidence to prove I ended the life of Blaine Davis without adequate legal cause. The digital recording my FBI phone made—not only of the audio but, son of a gun, also of some panoramic video, too—suggests rather blatantly that I continued to choke Blaine in order to kill him out of spite, rather than out of the need for self-defense.

"But the video was grainy," is how Harnischfeger puts it in the debriefing meeting he alone holds with me. "So what exists now in the Bureau's files is a report signed by me stating that my findings were inconclusive."

"Meaning what?" I ask.

"Meaning that, in this case, we presume self-defense."

"Meaning you're not going to arrest me?"

He nods. "Meaning you're free to go."

I search his steely eyes for some sort of hedge, some non-verbal prelude to a zinging, cynical statement about how I am in fact free to go back to my tidy little cell in Sing Sing.

But I find no such hedge.

He does, however, blink once, as if perfunctorily, before he says, "And remember: The Bureau never goes public with the identities of any undercover personnel, especially one who happened to kill a suspect in self-defense. For that matter, the Bureau will never let it be known that Matt Connell was part of this investigation in the first place."

I nod, still fearing a verbal hammer will strike.

"And of course," he says with a decisive nod, "the Bureau would require that you yourself keep everything you know about this investigation, your participation included, secret from everyone you know, with no exceptions for spouses or lovers or what have you. That is, if you want to leave open the possibility of going undercover for us again."

And that's it.

Those are the last words Carl Harnischfeger dispenses to me, leaving me with nothing to do but hand over my slick, shiny phone, shake hands with him, and exit those temporary headquarters in that huge, white marble library on Forty-First and Fifth.

I still have access to the place on Duane, though, I realize as I cab downtown. He didn't ask me to return the keys to it, so apparently, for a few more days, I still have its modest but clean and respectable square footage to use to reestablish myself as a literary agent who could sell the best unpublished manuscripts in the world.

I have not eaten since a chicken with pesto sandwich yesterday evening, so I ask the cabbie to drop me at my bodega, where, to celebrate my freedom, my new, unfettered freedom, I buy a few bags of blue corn chips, some guac dip, and three bottles of Pellegrino.

And it's a nice afternoon, I realize after I begin walking east. It's balmy. It's sunlit. It's summertime.

And when I round the corner onto the block on Duane I can still call mine, I see her:

Em.

Standing on my stoop, reaching for the button you need to press to be buzzed in.

"Heya," she calls when she notices me.

"Yo," I call back.

I neither accelerate nor slow down, and she stays put—in this regard, I believe, there is hope.

"Did you hear?" she says after I give her a little kiss.

"What?"

"They caught him."

"Who caught who?"

"The FBI. Caught the Talent Killer. And it was *Blaine* freaking *Davis*. And they offed him on the spot. I mean, he's dead, Matt. *Finis*. As in, your freakin' nemesis is *gone*."

I search her face for some sign that she knows more than she's letting on. I see none, but that doesn't mean there is none.

"Seriously?" I ask, and I let my jaw drop, as if I've been clueless.

"Seriously," she says, but on her face is a flash of the brightness that sent my mind whirring the moment we met, the same brightness I all but gave up on days ago, the brightness that still, despite my two major transgressions against the criminal laws of the State of New York, makes me feel as innocent as I was when I was fifteen.

I unlock the security door to the building, gesture for her to lead us in.

"How 'bout that," I say as she takes the first step up.

"Yeah," she says, turning to face me. "How 'bout that."

ACKNOWLEDGMENTS

Foremost thanks to publisher Jaynie Royal and editor Pam Van Dyk, for all your time and expertise. Heartfelt thanks to every bright-minded and generous novelist and poet I've met over the years—without your friendship, humor, anecdotes, and support, no way would this book be as much as drafted. Extra thanks to the talented authors in *Coolest American Stories*, for submitting manuscripts candid and engaging enough to assure me courageous storytelling can overcome political rancor. Special thanks to *The Iowa Review* for its timely publication of the poem "Hope" herein. And boundless thanks to Elizabeth, my partner in endless love, fun, adventure, and literary crime: E, there'd be no verve in this storyline without you.